MUTE

Lydia Wiebe

ISBN 978-1-64349-410-4 (paperback)
ISBN 978-1-64349-411-1 (digital)

Christian Faith Publishing, Inc.
832 Park Avenue
Meadville, PA 16335
www.christianfaithpublishing.com

Printed in the United States of America

Chapter 1

Lightning flashed and was followed by crashing thunder. Rain fell in angry torrents. Under the overpass, a silent group stood and watched the storm. They were an assorted group of people: a guitarist, a war veteran, and some drug addicts. All had one common denominator—they were homeless.

Off to one side sat a girl, staring listlessly at the group huddled under the overpass. She was a young girl of twelve, with dark brown eyes and a dark complexion. Her long brown hair, though once beautiful, was matted and tangled.

A man stumbled by and almost tripped over the girl. He grinned, revealing crooked yellow teeth. "What'cha doin' girlie?" he slurred. When she remained silent, he let out a loud guffaw and leaned closer. "What'sa matter? Cat got your tongue?"

"Leave her alone."

The man turned and peered through bleary eyes into the darkness to see who had given the command.

A young man materialized out of the darkness. He crossed his arms over his chest, prepared to back up his words with his fists, if necessary.

The old man shrugged and staggered on, mumbling under his breath.

Kyle Bennet turned and sat down beside his sister. "You okay, Riana?" he asked.

Riana nodded, relaxing because Kyle was with her. Three years older than her, Kyle had always been her protector.

The two sat in silence, and, together, they watched the rain fall.

*****

Kyle walked briskly along the street, Riana following close behind. They slipped quietly into the Taco Bell, attracting the disgusted looks of the few early morning patrons. This restaurant had served as their place to clean up for a couple of weeks now. So far none of the workers had had the nerve to tell them not to come back. It would happen yet. It always did. But until then, they would continue to come here.

"Hurry up," Kyle told Riana.

Riana nodded and quickly went into the women's restroom. Seconds later, a woman walked out, wrinkling her nose.

Kyle stepped into the men's restroom, which was empty, and proceeded to wash up. The water became a murky brown as he washed his arms and face. When you lived on the streets, you were never clean. It was a choice between dirty and dirtier. He splashed water on his face, then walked out to where Riana was waiting for him. They hurried out, away from the aroma of the food. There was no money for breakfast today. Hopefully, they could either earn enough money for lunch or scrounge something up from the garbage cans.

*****

Autumn walked into class a few minutes before the bell and slid into the seat next to Savannah.

Savannah looked up from her frantic cramming to whisper a quick "Hey."

Autumn chuckled. "Didn't do your studying last night?"

Savannah narrowed her eyes at Autumn, but only for a moment before breaking into a grin.

Savannah and Autumn, almost sixteen-year-olds, had been best friends for as long as they could remember, so Autumn took no offense at Savannah's glare.

Just then the bell rang and in swished Miss Reims.

"Good morning, class. I hope you are ready for the exam today." She turned abruptly to face the class. "But before we begin, I have an announcement to make. Since Thanksgiving is coming up, our class will be making a trip to the homeless shelter."

A collective groan came up from all areas of the class, but Miss Reims continued, "I've already cleared it with your parents. We'll be going to the shelter at ten forty-five on Wednesday. You'll each be given a specific job to do while we are there. Are there any questions?"

Cynthia Rowl, a cheerleader and one of the most popular girls in school, raised her hand. "I have a question, Miss Reims. Do we, like, have to go? Or is this optional? Because homeless shelters stink, and I really don't want to ruin my reputation."

Cynthia's friends tittered at this last comment.

"No, this is not optional," Miss Reims said, "though I highly doubt your reputation will be hurt by showing some kindness to those who have less than us. Anyone who fails to show up will be given an automatic zero, as well as having detention. Furthermore, after we are finished with the assignment, you will each be required to write an essay on some of the many things you have to be thankful for. I'm sure you'll have lots to write about."

"I'll be thankful when this stupid assignment is over," muttered Toby Fraser.

If Miss Reims heard him, she chose to ignore his remark. "Now, if you will all get out a pencil and a sheet of paper."

Chapter 2

The wind was chilly and blew right through Kyle's thin jacket. He glanced at Riana, who was standing on the other side of the street. Hopefully, she was having more success than he was. Again, he raised his sign, which stated, "Homeless. Hungry. Anything helps."

Normally, winter weather and the upcoming holidays put people in a more generous mood, but, today, everyone seemed to be in too much of a hurry to get somewhere and didn't have time for beggars.

Even from where Kyle was standing, he could see that Riana was shivering. She needed a new jacket, but at the moment, they didn't even have enough money for a decent meal. It hurt, knowing he couldn't provide for her needs. For as long as he could remember, he had been Riana's protector. The day she was born he had appointed himself as her guardian. And when Riana turned three and still couldn't talk, he protected her from anyone who might make fun of her. The doctors had given it a fancy word, but to Kyle it only meant that Riana would never speak. Though they were older now, Kyle still felt the need to protect her. It was then that Kyle decided that drastic measures were necessary.

*****

The Shays were sitting at the supper table when Autumn brought up the subject of the Thanksgiving project.

"That sounds interesting," Dad said.

Mom smiled knowingly. "How did your class react to that?"

"Most of them can't stand the thought of it, and I've heard a lot of complaining." Autumn shrugged. "I can't say I'm too excited about it myself. I mean, I feel sorry for them and everything, but going to a homeless shelter . . . I don't know. It just seems kind of weird."

Mom gave Autumn a measuring look. "You know what? I think this is exactly what you need."

"Why do you say that?"

"Autumn, you need to put your faith into action. How closely are you really following Jesus's footsteps?"

Autumn shifted uncomfortably. "Well, I do want to help those who don't have as much as we do, but couldn't we just give a donation or something?"

"Giving, if it comes from the heart, is good, but Jesus didn't just give us salvation while sitting on his throne in heaven. He came down to earth and He walked among men. He ate with tax collectors and sinners, and He even cast demons out of the demon-possessed. Shouldn't you also be willing to walk among those less fortunate than us?"

Ashamed, Autumn dropped her head. "You're right," she assented.

"Of course, your mother is right," Dad said. "She's always right. Well, except for the time on our honeymoon when we were on our way to the airport. We were running a bit late for our flight to the romantic beach hideaway we were going to in Hawaii, so your mom pointed out a shortcut that would get us there quicker." He paused for dramatic effect. "It turned out to be a shortcut that took longer than the original route would have, and we ended up missing our flight." Dad reclined in his chair and hooked his hands behind his head. "Come to think of it, there was also that time at the circus."

"Andrew."

There was a warning tone in Mom's voice, but Dad chose to ignore it.

"We were married about a year at the time, and your mom loved circuses. So when there was a big circus in town, she insisted that we go."

Autumn looked at Mom with raised eyebrows. It was hard to imagine Mom, an ER doctor, as a person who would enjoy circuses.

Dad continued his story. "We were looking for the House of Mirrors, and I made the mistake of letting your mom lead the way. Well, you know how she is with directions. We got lost before we got there. We ended up in the area where a bunch of tents were set up." Dad grinned at Mom. "Mom decided it would be a good idea to ask somebody for directions, and what do you know, she ends up asking a clown, who, instead of answering her, grabs her arm and pulls her into a tent. I was ready to run in after her and save her from the evil clown, but another clown informed me that they were just in need of another clown. She wouldn't need to do anything just slip on a banana peel, get up, and get splatted on the face with a cream pie by another clown who just happened to ride by on a tricycle."

Autumn laughed incredulously, as Dad described how Mom looked in a clown costume, with colorful hair, and a red nose. "Even then, you were beautiful, Maureen," he said, looking at her lovingly.

"I can't believe you let them do that to Mom," Autumn said, still laughing.

"Well, I did have a choice," Mom said.

"What?"

"They wouldn't have been able to force somebody to join their act," Mom said, smiling at Autumn's astonishment. "When they asked me to help them out, I agreed."

"Wow," was all Autumn could say.

"Mom was a little more adventurous when she was younger," Dad teased.

"What happened to change that?" Autumn asked her Mom.

"You were born," Mom said in a dry tone of voice. "I couldn't handle any more adventure than that."

The banter continued a little while longer before Autumn excused herself to do her homework.

Chapter 3

As Autumn readied herself for bed, she thought back to what her parents had said. She knew they were right. You need to do more than say you are following Christ. You need to show it in your life. But, though she didn't approve of Cynthia's way of expressing it, Cynthia had a point. Autumn had seen her share of homeless people. Living in a big city like Larem, Kansas, gave ample opportunity to see them. Sometimes, Mom would stop and give them a bottle of water or some small bills. Wasn't that enough?

Autumn walked to her bedroom and looked for a moment at the Bible on her nightstand, before turning out the light. She was much too tired to stay up any longer. She would just read her Bible tomorrow.

Twenty minutes later, Autumn lay wide awake, unable to fall asleep. She knew full well what the reason was. Rolling out of bed, she dropped to her knees.

"Father," she prayed, "I'm sorry for having a bad attitude about our project. I keep trying to justify myself by telling myself I'm not as bad as the other children from school, but I know that's not true. I'm not supposed to compare myself to how they act but to how You want me to act. You care for all the people without homes, so help me to have a heart for them too. In Jesus's name, Amen."

Slipping into bed once more, Autumn fell asleep only a few minutes later.

*****

Hunger woke Riana. Yesterday had been a poor day for panhandling, and there had been only what little they could rummage up from the garbage cans for supper. A quick glance around her told her that Kyle was already up.

A few other people who had bedded under the bridge straggled about. Some were strangers, the kind that traveled from place to place. Others were familiar, such as the older couple, who lost all their money in a bad financial investment. Nobody knew their names and they said little. Then there was Rodney, a drug addict, who lost his job as a result of his addictions. He was really nice, when he wasn't high.

Riana didn't see Kyle among the people still there. Where was he? Riana sighed in frustration. It was difficult not being able to talk to people. The pad and pencil Kyle had gotten for her had long since been used up. The fact that she knew he had stolen it used to bother her, but now it was just a fact of life. You did what you had to, to survive.

Kyle appeared from around the corner of the bridge. He was breathing hard, and, upon seeing Riana's quizzical expression, he said, "I was looking to see if I could find some breakfast."

His empty hands answered her next question. Without another word, he motioned, and the two of them walked silently to Taco Bell.

Inside Taco Bell, a man wearing a name tag that said manager, stood, waiting for them. And, again, they were turned out.

*****

The Thanksgiving project was fast approaching. Most people grumbled and complained. Cynthia and her friends never missed a chance to mention how gross they thought it was.

Autumn still wasn't sure about the project, but she felt assurance that God was going to bless it.

*****

Kyle slipped into the dark alley and let his eyes adjust. No one was here yet. He sat down to wait. Looking behind himself one more time, he made sure Riana hadn't followed him. It was always tough getting away from her. Leaving while she was asleep was hard enough, but in broad daylight, it was nearly impossible.

Kyle shifted impatiently. He was sure this was the place he had been told to come to. A few more minutes passed, and he was getting antsy. He was about ready to leave, when three dark figures appeared.

"You're such a brave man to show up." There was a sneer in the man's voice. He was a big man, so big it looked like he could easily snap someone in two, and his skin was a charcoal black, making him almost disappear in the dark alleyway.

Kyle tried to make his voice sound equally tough when in reality he was shaking. "You're late," he said.

Derek shot the boy a hard look. "Now, see here. I ain't ever late. I show up when I want to, I come only if I want to, and I leave when I want to, but I ain't ever late. You got that?"

Kyle nodded, trying to hide his fear.

"Now, why did you come to see me this morning?" Derek asked.

"I need money. Cold, hard cash."

Derek raised an eyebrow condescendingly. "Begging ain't working out for you?"

Kyle clenched his fists but held back his anger. "I know you're rolling in the dough, and I want in. I can help you out and you can help me out."

Derek stared at him long and hard. Abruptly, he turned to one of his comrades and held out his hand. A bag of white powder was placed in it.

"I happen to be in need of another distributor in your part of town. But I need someone I can trust. Someone who won't snitch or chicken out. We don't take kindly to traitors."

Kyle nodded. "I can handle it."

Again Kyle was under Derek's scrutiny. "We'll see about that," he said. "I will give you one job. If you can handle it, we'll give you the official initiation, and it'll be well worth your while. If you mess this up . . ."

A few minutes later, Kyle turned to leave with several white packets and strict instructions. Just as he was about to walk away, Derek's voice stopped him.

"How's your sister?"

Kyle stiffened. "Leave my sister out of this!"

"Now, that is entirely up to you." Derek chuckled. "You just remember that. It's all up to you."

Chapter 4

The students were strangely silent as they boarded the bus to go to the homeless shelter. As much as everyone had dreaded it, the day had arrived.

Autumn and Savannah sat together at the back of the bus. They rode in silence. In fact, all was quiet, except for a few nervous giggles from the girls. As everyone climbed out of the bus, the long lines in front of the homeless shelter surprised Autumn. Young and old alike stood there, some staring blankly, others shuffling slowly, and yet others hanging their heads in shame. All their eyes spoke of despair and hopelessness.

"I didn't realize there were so many homeless people," Savannah whispered to Autumn.

Autumn could only nod her head in agreement.

Once inside, everyone was quickly assigned their jobs. Autumn was told to hand out bread and given strict instructions not to give anyone more than two pieces.

The lady in charge said, "Some people will give you a sob story to try to get you to give them more, but don't give in. They likely won't make a fuss, but if they do, someone will be around to help you out. Just remember, if you start to give people more than their allotted amount, we may not have enough food for all the others in line."

Autumn had quickly agreed. It sounded easy enough. But, as she soon found out, it was not as easy as it sounded. Almost everyone looked like they could use more food. She tried to offer each person a smile and an encouraging word, but they had an empty ring to them when all these people wanted was food.

One young lady, with a baby whose eyes were sunken and hollow, walked up. As Autumn put the allotted amount on her tray, the lady spoke up. "Miss, I got a baby and two other young'uns. Couldn't you just give me some more for my chil'run?"

Autumn hesitated, then looked at the long line of people still waiting for food. "I'm sorry, ma'am. That's all I can give you. There are others who need food as well."

The woman straightened and turned away without another word.

"May God bless you," Autumn called after her. Her heart ached for the young mother.

With a sigh, Autumn turned back to the line of people. Big brown eyes stared up at her, silently asking for food. Smiling, Autumn placed the bread on the girl's tray. "What's your name?" she asked.

The girl only smiled. A clearing of the throat reminded Autumn that others were waiting. As she placed the bread on the next tray, she looked up into a young man's face. Startled, she gasped. A large gash stood open on the side of his head, and his left eye was an ugly purple color. Instinctively, she reached up to touch it. "What happened?"

The boy stepped back quickly, pulling out of her reach. "It's nothing. My bread, please?"

Autumn put the bread on his tray, and he turned quickly to walk away. "C'mon, Riana."

The girl followed silently.

Autumn glanced around helplessly, then turned to Cynthia, who was serving beside her. "Could you take over here for a minute?"

"You can't just shirk on your duties," Cynthia protested. "I am not—"

Autumn hurried away, leaving Cynthia and her tirade behind. She scanned the room, looking for the two children. She spotted them just as they reached the door. Dodging trays and people, she dashed toward them. When she reached the door, she called, "Wait!"

The two turned around and looked at her suspiciously.

"What do you want?" the boy asked.

Autumn took a deep breath. What did she want? What had made her run after them? She wasn't rightly sure, but here she was.

Finding her voice, she said, "That cut on your head. It needs to be cleaned up and bandaged. Otherwise it could get infected."

The look the boy gave her was one of absolute scorn. "Why should you care? Just so you can get it off your conscience? You feel guilty because of what you see in there." He gestured to the homeless shelter. "But you'll go back to your warm home and family, feeling like you did something good. Well, let me tell you something. Outside of your fairy-tale life, there's the real world. Out here, we fend for ourselves. We don't need your help, so just forget it." With that, he grabbed his sister's hand, and they disappeared around a corner, leaving Autumn still fumbling for an answer.

*****

Kyle smiled in satisfaction at Riana's delight as she tried on her new jacket. What would have taken months to earn just begging had been earned in only a week's time working for Derek. The pain he had went through during his initiation, as Derek called it, had been well worth it. He reflected on Derek's words to him after the pounding he had received from the rest of the gang.

"You're part of our family now. People call us a gang, but that's not really what we are. We're family. Just remember this. Family helps each other out, and never, ever snitches." Then as an afterthought, he had added, "The pain you felt just now, is nothing compared to the pain a snitch will feel."

Kyle chuckled dryly as he thought about the girl from the homeless shelter. She had made quite a picture, running after them, apron flying in the wind, because she was concerned about the cut on his face. "She's forgotten us by now, I'm sure," he said to himself.

Chapter 5

Kyle was wrong. Autumn had by no means forgotten them. In fact, she thought about them all the time.

"I don't know why it bothers me so much," Autumn confided in her parents one day. "That kind of stuff probably goes on all the time, and, like he said, they take care of themselves."

"It bothers you," Mom said, "because God has put it on your heart. There is a reason for that. You may not know the reason now, and you may never know what it is, but you need to pray for those two children because God is prompting you to."

Dad added his insight with these words. "Pray also that if God wants you to do something, He will show you what to do. There is a time to take action and a time to just pray."

Autumn took these words to heart, and every night could be found on her knees, praying not only for the two children, but for all the people she had seen at the homeless shelter.

*****

Riana awoke to find herself alone again.

Riana sighed. Kyle would never tell her where he was going. He just said it was for her good.

She shook her head. She didn't like this one bit. She was pretty sure he was involved in something illegal. First, he comes back with his face all battered and bleeding, then he starts slipping away during the night and coming back with money.

Stealing food, when necessary, was one thing but getting involved in something big was completely another. What if he got caught or hurt or . . . or . . .

Riana didn't want to think about it. All she knew was that Kyle was risking her life and it was all her fault.

*****

"Good morning," Autumn greeted Savannah as they met at their lockers.

Her only answer was the slamming of the locker door before Savannah stalked away.

Bewildered, Autumn grabbed her books out of the locker, and then ran to catch up with her.

"Wait up," she called after her friend.

Savannah stopped but didn't turn around.

"What's wrong?" Autumn said to her back. "Did I do something? Or say something? Savannah, please tell me what's wrong!"

Now she turned around. "What's wrong? I'll tell you what's wrong. I called my best friend twice yesterday, and both times, she cut me off short and told me she would call me back later. Guess what? She never did. It's been days since our trip to the homeless shelter, Autumn, and yet you're still so caught up with that, that you don't have any time for your friends. The Christmas season is coming up and I've been wanting to go shopping with you, but you keep brushing me off. But," She turned to walk away, "other than that everything is fine and dandy."

"Savannah," Autumn began but was interrupted by the bell. She watched helplessly as Savannah disappeared in a mass of students on their way to class. With a sigh, she too hurried to get to class.

*****

It was lunchtime before Autumn had the chance to talk to Savannah again.

Sliding into the seat across from her, Autumn said, "Savannah, I need to apologize."

"I'm listening."

"Well, first of all, I'm sorry for not returning your calls yesterday. And I'm sorry for not going shopping with you. And I'm sorry for being so wrapped up in my problems." Autumn took a deep breath. "But I have been thinking a lot about all those people we saw at the homeless shelter. I wish I could do something for them."

"I feel sorry for them, too," Savannah said, "but I'm not letting that ruin my life."

Autumn frowned. "It's not ruining my life. It's making me rethink my life. Why spend so much money on myself or even shopping for others when others are going hungry. I could be using my money for better purposes."

"Well, have fun rethinking your life," Savannah said. "I'm going to ask Miranda if she wants to go shopping with me on Saturday." With that, she picked up her lunch tray and moved to a nearby table where a group of girls was talking and giggling.

"That went well," Autumn muttered. She shoved her tray away. Somehow, the hamburger didn't taste as good when eating it by yourself.

Chapter 6

Huddling in a corner, trying to keep out of the wind, Riana sat waiting for Kyle to come back with lunch. As she sat there, she let her mind drift back to a time when it had been Mama, Daddy, Kyle, and her. She could vaguely remember happy times. Daddy holding her on his lap while Mama smiled, and Kyle played on the floor nearby.

But then, things changed. Mama and Daddy had started arguing all the time. The fights normally ended with Daddy storming out of the house, declaring that he needed a pick-me-up. Mama would sit there and cry.

Riana had hoped the fights would stop, but they only escalated. Riana and Kyle started hiding in their rooms until Daddy left. And then one day, Daddy just didn't come back.

Things only went downhill from there.

One day, when Riana was five, Mama got a phone call that left her in tears. After she got off the phone, she explained to Kyle and Riana that they were going to move out of their house and go live somewhere else.

So they left the only home they had ever known, along with all the good memories it contained, and moved into the shack they were to call home for the next two years.

While they were living there, Mama developed a horrible cough. It started slowly, but eventually left Mama bedridden.

Because Mama couldn't work, they were always short on money. Every month, a check, which Mama called alimony, would come in the mail, but it was barely enough to give them the bare necessities.

The neighbors helped them out where they could, but most of them were almost as bad off as they were.

The lack of nourishment left Mama worse off than ever before. She continued to tell the children she would get better. "There's no need to call a doctor and get more bills," she said when Kyle suggested it. Under her breath, she muttered, "Heaven knows, we have enough bills."

But instead of getting better, as she insisted she would, Mama only got worse. Finally, out of desperation, Kyle took matters into his own hands.

It had been a cold, rainy day, and Mama's cough was very bad. By Kyle's reasoning, if she could get some medicine, she would get better. So he decided to get some for her. The only problem was that the security camera at the drugstore caught him trying to smuggle it out of the store.

It took an hour of trying to sort things out, Kyle trying to explain that his mom was sick and needed medicine, that they didn't have a phone, and that they didn't know where his dad was. Finally, a police officer drove Kyle back home. Seeing the condition Mama was in, he didn't even bother to tell her why he had to bring Kyle over in his police car. He simply called an ambulance, despite her protests.

As the paramedics loaded Mama onto the stretcher, she gave Kyle one more look and said, "When I get back home, I want you tell me the whole story about what happened today."

The police officer took the children to the hospital and waited with them to hear news about Mama.

It seemed like hours before a doctor finally appeared.

"Your mom is very sick," he told them. "She has lung cancer." Seeing the children's confused faces, he quickly clarified, "A sickness in her throat. She needs to stay here so we can help her get better."

It was arranged for Kyle and Riana to stay at a neighbor's house until Mama got better. But Mama didn't get better. Only a few weeks later, she died. Her smoking and the delay before going to the hospital had cost her her life.

After the funeral, a lady named Miss Fin drove them home and told them to pack all their things. They would be going with her.

Kyle took Riana's hand and led her to the room they shared. They quickly packed their meager belongings, but instead of returning to the front room where Miss Fin was waiting, they slipped quietly out the window into the night.

As they made their escape, Kyle explained to Riana the reason for their flight. "Miss Fin is a social worker," he said. "And she would take us to a different place to live called a foster home. She would separate us. But I'm not going to let that happen. I'll take care of you."

He had kept his promise. And now he was getting into something risky, so he could take care of her, when meanwhile, it was all her fault.

Riana knew that if Kyle had any idea what she was thinking, he would quickly inform her that she was wrong. But she knew better.

Their life had been good until they found out that Riana would never speak. That's when Daddy had started drinking. That's when Mama had started smoking. That's when Mama and Daddy had started fighting. One argument in particular stood out in Riana's memory.

Riana was supposed to be sleeping, but she heard Daddy get home and wanted to give him a hug. As she got closer, she heard angry voices. At first, she couldn't distinguish the words, but the voices got louder.

"She's your child too," Mama shouted. "You can help pay the bills!"

"I never counted on having a dumb kid," Daddy retorted. "And we wouldn't have all those bills if you hadn't insisted on going to all those stupid specialists!"

The voices receded, and it wasn't long before the door slammed, signaling Daddy's departure.

And that's how Riana knew. The fights, the doctor bills, Daddy's drinking, the loss of the house, and Mama's death—all of it was her fault.

Chapter 7

"She's so frustrating!" Autumn spouted. She had spent the rest of the day feeling miserable, and now her pent-up feelings came spilling out. "She acts like she doesn't even care about the homeless. All she wanted to do was talk about shopping. Shopping of all things! Like any of us need new things. And then she had the nerve to say that I was letting this ruin my life." Autumn slapped her hand on the table. "She is so self-centered!"

Autumn's parents let her finish her tirade before interjecting.

"Maybe," Dad said, choosing his words carefully, "there is a bit of truth to what Savannah said."

"You think I'm overreacting?" Autumn couldn't believe what she was hearing. She had expected her parents to be understanding, and now Dad was agreeing with Savannah?

"Honey, God has given you a caring and sensitive heart," Dad said, "and we believe God has placed this on your heart for a reason. Maybe He is calling you to do something, maybe He just wants you to pray. But you can't just sit on your hands waiting to see if God wants you to do something. You may miss out on part of His plan for your life if you do."

"What do you mean?"

"If you always stay home, you may miss out on an opportunity to serve God in other ways," Dad explained. "And there is nothing wrong with having a little fun with your friends."

"But it just seems so wrong," Autumn said. "None of my friends understand why I feel so strongly about this."

Mom chuckled. "Autumn, remember that summer when Savannah got into bugs."

"I remember," Autumn laughed. "We were seven, and Savannah suddenly decided that bugs were 'cool.'"

"Yup. And the two of you would tramp all over our backyard in search of anything wiggly. If ever I saw Savannah animatedly talking, I could guarantee she was talking about her bug collection. She loved bugs, but you—"

"I was terrified of them," Autumn interrupted, laughing.

"If you were terrified of them, why did you put up with it?" Mom asked.

"Because we were best friends."

"Exactly," Mom said with a smile. "Savannah may not have the passion for the homeless that you do, but this isn't the first time you haven't had the same interests. And it's never changed your friendship before. There's no need for it to change now. I'm sure Savannah will be willing to listen to your interests, but don't forget it goes both ways. You need to be willing to listen to her as well."

"You're right, again," Autumn smiled ruefully. "I guess I have been so stuck on this that I haven't really taken the time to listen to Savannah." Standing up, she said, "I think I'll go call her right now."

But Savannah didn't pick up the phone.

"I guess I'll have to talk to her tomorrow," Autumn sighed.

*****

Savannah was not waiting at the lockers the next morning. Autumn looked around and spotted her friend standing by Miranda's locker. They were talking and laughing. It looked like they were having a great time.

"I'll talk to her at lunch," Autumn decided.

But lunchtime found Savannah already surrounded by other girls. Autumn joined them, but knew it was not the time to bring up the subject that was on her mind.

The rest of the day slipped away, never giving Autumn the opportunity to talk one on one with Savannah.

"Tomorrow," Autumn thought.

It didn't take long for it to become painfully clear that Savannah was avoiding her. She was always either busy or with other people.

It was Friday when Autumn decided she'd had enough. Marching up to where Savannah was eating lunch, Autumn asked, "Can I talk to you, Savannah?"

"Sure," Savannah said, but made no move to get up.

"In private," Autumn prompted and motioned to an empty table that was nearby.

Savannah got up with obvious reluctance and followed Autumn. "What do you want?"

Autumn hesitated a moment, not quite sure how to start. She decided to use her mom's approach. "Savannah, do you remember the summer you were obsessed with bugs?"

"I wasn't obsessed," Savannah protested. "I just liked them a lot."

"And talked about them all the time, had bug collections, researched them, decided to become a 'bug scientist,' and even tried to train one?"

Savannah smiled grudgingly. "Well, maybe I was a little obsessed."

"A little? Girl, when you try to train a bug, you know you are more than a little overboard."

Cocking an eyebrow, Savannah said, "At least, I wasn't terrified of them like you were."

"It's called bug phobia," Autumn said, "and many people are afflicted with it."

"Right," Savannah said, then smiled. "Remember that time you knocked over my ant collection? There were ants everywhere, and you were screaming and jumping around, terrified out of your mind."

Laughing, Autumn added, "If I remember correctly, you were also screaming. Something like, 'Don't step on my ants! Stay away! They're just as scared of you as you are of them!'"

"I lost thirteen ants that day," Savannah said, pretending to shed a tear. Then growing serious, she said, "So you wanted to talk about bugs?"

24

"Well, Mom reminded me of that summer the day after our disagreement," Autumn said. "She asked me why I put up with it. I told her it was because you were my best friend. Our differences didn't keep us from being best friends then and I don't think they should now. I know I've thought a lot about the people from the homeless shelter since Thanksgiving, and I've kinda expected you to share my enthusiasm about it. When you didn't, I got upset. I'm sorry about that. Will you forgive me?"

"I don't know," Savannah said, then paused. "I guess I have to since you put up with my bug fever."

Both girls laughed.

After a moment of comfortable silence, Savannah said, "Hey, do you want to go shopping with us tomorrow?"

"Will Miranda mind if I come along?"

"No, I'm sure she won't," Savannah said. "She invited Kaylee to come, too, so we could make it a foursome."

"I'll have to ask my parents, but I'll let you know this evening," Autumn promised.

Chapter 8

Kyle strode down the dimly-lit street. The early morning sun was just beginning to brighten the horizon, promising a beautiful sunrise, but he was in too much of a hurry to notice. He quickly turned a corner into a dark alley between two brick buildings. The dreariness of the alley was a sharp contrast to the beauty of the sky. Beer bottles littered the ground, graffiti colored the walls, and the stench of cigarette smoke filled the air.

All the way at the back of the alley, Kyle squatted down beside the wall. Making sure he was blocked from the view of any passersby, he removed a loose brick. In the hollow behind it was a bag of money. Kyle switched the money for the small bag of powder, stashed the money in his pocket, and quickly replaced the brick. Every week, he came to make the exchange. He didn't know who he was delivering drugs to, but it didn't really make a difference. He brought the coke, got the money, and brought the money to Derek, who gave him his share. As long as they got paid, nothing else mattered.

Lately, Derek had been talking about something big. "You're just doin' the little stuff," he said, "but keep it up, and you can get where the real dough is."

Kyle was thinking about this as he rounded the corner. In fact, he was so absorbed in his thoughts that he didn't see the police officer until he almost bumped into him.

Kyle's heart sped up. It was too late to run, and that would just cause suspicion anyway.

"It's pretty early for a boy like you to be out," the officer commented casually.

Trying to keep his cool, Kyle answered, "I like to take a walk first thing in the morning, when there's not so many people out."

"In an alley?"

Kyle thought fast. "Well, sir, my sister's cat ran away last week. I heard a noise in the alley, and I thought maybe it was Snowball. But it was just a big rat."

The office was clearly skeptical, but said, "Well, good luck in finding your cat."

"Thank you, sir," Kyle said, then turned and walked away. As he rounded the corner, he let out a sigh of relief. That was close. Too close. If the officer had caught him putting the coke behind the brick, he would've been a goner.

*****

Daniel Quinn had been a law enforcement officer for too long to be fooled by this kid.

Walking back to his car, he opened the door and addressed his partner, Mark Wenger. "Let's search that alley."

"You think that kid is part of the drug smugglers?" Mark asked.

"Only one way to find out," Daniel said, as the two of them walked to the alley.

*****

"What were you thinking!"

Kyle gasped for breath. As soon as he had walked into the house where he always brought the money after an exchange, Derek had grabbed him by the collar and shoved him against the wall. Then, just as suddenly as he had been grabbed, he was released.

Derek began pacing, still glaring at Kyle. "Our costumer went to pick up his package, and what should he see but two cops standing watch. They were trying to act casual, but he could tell they were watching the alley where the exchange is always made. He had no way of getting his package. How did the cops find out that that was where we kept it?" He turned on his heel. "Why where you not

27

watching your back? No one should have seen you go in there. And now we have a very unhappy costumer."

"I-I'm sorry, Derek," Kyle stammered. He had been scared when he ran into the police officer, but that didn't compare to the fear he felt when facing Derek. "I'm pretty sure there was no one around when I went in there. By the time I seen him, it was too late." He swallowed hard. "I can see if I can get back in there and check if the stuff is still there."

"No," Derek said. "We can't risk you getting caught. We'll need to find another distribution point." Pointing a finger at Kyle, he said, "You make another mistake like that and you're out. You got that?"

"Yeah."

"We can't risk messing things up now," Derek said. "We've got a big deal coming up. If you want to be part of it, you'd better shape up."

Kyle was relieved to hear that Derek hadn't eliminated him from the big deal. The longer he was in the business, the more addicted he became to the profit from the business he was in. He didn't want to go back to begging on street corners. It didn't make nearly as much money, and from when they had started out on their own, there had always been the fear that they would be picked up and brought to social services. Since it had been years ago, the fear had diminished a little, but it was never completely gone.

"I'll be careful," Kyle promised.

Derek, watching him go, was sure he would be. Kyle was a clever boy, and Derek felt he could go far. In fact, he thought that maybe Kyle could get to the top one day.

Chapter 9

Autumn, Savannah, Miranda, and Kaylee sat at the table in the mall's food court.

"I can't believe how crowded it is in here," Kaylee commented, as she munched on a fry.

"I know," Savannah said. "It's always like this close to the holidays, but it never ceases to amaze me how crowded it gets."

"I'm just glad we're doing our shopping now and not closer to Christmas. It'll only get more crowded from here on," Miranda said.

Savannah glanced at Autumn with an amused look in her eye. "What are you thinking about?"

"Oh," Autumn said, "I just got an idea, but never mind."

"It's about the homeless people, right?" Savannah asked.

"Yes, but I won't bore you with the details."

"Homeless people?" Miranda asked.

"What are you talking about?" Kaylee added.

"Well, ever since our project for Miss Riems's class, Autumn has been wanting to help the homeless people," Savannah said. Then, turning back to Autumn, she said, "Okay, I'm ready to hear your idea."

"Do you really want to hear it or would you rather talk about something else?"

"We definitely want to hear what you have to say," Kaylee said. "I've been wanting to do something for them, but I didn't know what I could do. So if you have any suggestions, I would love to hear them."

The other girls nodded their agreement.

"Okay," Autumn said, "here's my idea. With everyone getting new stuff this time of year, people will all most likely be wanting to clean out their closets to make room for all their new stuff."

"So?"

"So we could have a clothing drive and collect clothes for the people who don't have enough," Autumn said, now warming onto her subject. "I could even talk with the lady at the homeless shelter and ask her what other items would be good things to collect. We could put up posters and maybe even get some stores to donate stuff. Maybe we could ask the school if we could use the gymnasium as the place to bring all the stuff."

All the girls seemed to have caught Autumn's enthusiasm.

"We could ask my dad if he would put out an announcement on his radio program," Kaylee said.

"Kaylee, that's a great idea!" Autumn said. "I forgot that your dad works at the local radio station."

Miranda leaned forward a bit. "I think quite a few of the other girls would like to help with getting this organized. Maybe even some of the guys."

"Just one thing," Savannah said. "I don't think we should get any credit for this."

All the girls turned to look at her.

"What do you mean?" asked Kaylee.

"Well, I just don't think we should do this to be the center of attention or so that other people will notice us." She shrugged. "I just think that would ruin part of the point of doing this."

"You're right, Savannah," Autumn said. "I guess it goes along with the Bible verse where Jesus says not to let your right hand know what your left hand is doing. Or something like that."

Kaylee giggled. "It's actually the opposite. 'Let not your left hand know what your right hand is doing.' You should remember that. We learned it in Sunday school not long ago."

Autumn laughed ruefully. All four girls attended the same church and were in the same Sunday school class. "You have always been better at memorizing than me," she admitted.

After a bit more discussion, it was decided that they would all make sure it was okay with their parents, and on Monday, they would meet in the cafeteria and discuss it further.

With this decision made, they went back to their shopping.

*****

Monday, the girls met with the news that all their parents were game with their project.

"Dad said he'll do an announcement on his radio station," Kaylee said, "and he said he'd help out any way he could."

"And my mom said that she'll drive me over to the homeless shelter after school today to talk to the director there about any other needs they may have," Autumn said. "Dad suggested that we use the shelter as our distribution point, because they would know how to get the clothes and other items out to those who need it."

"Now, we just need someone to talk to the principal and see if we can use the gym for this," Savannah said.

Her comment was met with silence.

"Uumm," Miranda said, "I would offer to do that except that my relationship with the principal isn't the best."

The girls all nodded. Before Miranda had become a Christian, she was a frequent patron of the principal's office and was known for her disrespect of all in authority.

"Okay," Savannah sighed. "I guess I'll do it."

"Great!" Autumn said. "Make sure you confirm that December 20 would work. Since school will be out by then, it shouldn't make a difference that it's not a Saturday. And once we get that arranged, we can get started on making posters."

"I can buy all the supplies for that," Miranda offered.

"And we can make them at our house," said Kaylee. "Mom loves having people over, and I could probably convince her to make some cookies and hot chocolate to eat while we're working."

"Oh, that sounds good."

The bell cut their meeting off short, and they all rushed to get to class on time.

*****

After school, Autumn jumped into Mom's vehicle.

"Ready to go?" Mom asked.

"Yup."

"I called the shelter and got an appointment to talk to the director," Mom said.

"I didn't even realize you needed an appointment," Autumn said. "I'm glad you knew. Thanks."

The closer they got to the shelter, the more nervous Autumn became. "What if she doesn't think this is a good idea?" she asked when the homeless shelter came into view.

"She will think it's a good idea."

"But what if she doesn't want to talk to a high schooler. She'd probably rather have an adult planning this."

"Honey," Mom laid her hand on Autumn's knee. "When you told Dad and me about this plan, you were excited and said that you had finally found what God wanted you to do, right?"

Autumn nodded.

"Then it doesn't matter what the director here thinks now, does it?"

Autumn smiled gratefully at her Mom. "Thanks for reminding me of that," she said. Grabbing her notebook, she said, "Okay, I'm ready now."

The director was Miss Marlin, the same lady who had been giving the students assignments when the class had been there. She had a bit of a brusque manner and a very stern face. "What can I do for you?" she asked, directing the question at Mom.

Mom smiled encouragingly at Autumn, who cleared her throat nervously.

"Ma'am, I'm Autumn Shay, one of the students who were here on Thanksgiving," she began.

"I remember."

"Well, ever since then, I've wondered if there was some other way of helping. Some of my friends and I came up with an idea and I was hoping you could maybe help us out a bit."

"Okay."

Autumn licked her lips. "We're wanting to do some type of clothing drive, and we were hoping you could help us come up with suggestions to give to people, like, what type of things to bring. Of course, we'd ask for warm clothing, but what else is there that is needed?"

"Well, now," a small smile crept onto the woman's stern exterior. "That's the kind of thing we like to hear. There's a lot that's needed. Warm clothing would definitely be at the top of the list, blankets and pillows, too. Shoes, socks, even some toys would be greatly appreciated. Children suffer a lot when they're homeless."

Autumn nodded, a picture of the homeless shelter at Thanksgiving and all those hopeless faces flashed in her mind. "Anything else?"

"Those would be the main needs," Miss Marlin said. "How are you planning to distribute the items you get?"

"We were hoping you could help us out there too," Autumn said. "Since you would know more about where the needs are the greatest, would it be possible for us to bring the clothing and stuff here? We would be willing to help with distributing, but would you be willing to help us with knowing who to bring it to?"

This time a real smile peaked through. "Miss Shay," Miss Marlin said, holding out her hand, "I do believe we have a deal."

Chapter 10

That evening, Savannah called Autumn. "Principal Sterling was all for it," she said excitedly. "He even said that he would be there to help with all the organizing the clothes and everything. Can you imagine that! Principal Sterling is going to help us with our clothing drive." Then she quickly added, "I also told him that we didn't want anyone knowing who was in charge of the clothing drive. He said he understood and wouldn't tell anyone."

"Miss Marlin also agreed with our plan," Autumn said. "She'll help us distribute the stuff and everything."

"That's good," Savannah said. "By the way, Kaylee said her house is open for tomorrow, if we want to do the posters then."

"The sooner the better. We need to get word out to everyone as soon as possible."

They ended their conversation quickly.

*****

The next day, Miranda, Autumn, and Savannah met at their usual table in the cafeteria.

"Where's Kaylee?" Autumn asked. "I want everyone here so we can wrap up all the plans."

"Kaylee's often late," Miranda said, "but I'm sure she'll be here soon."

As if on cue, Kaylee walked up and plopped her tray onto the table. "Well," she said as she sat down, "we have failed miserably at keeping this thing a secret. I just ran into Genavieve in the hallway.

You know, the newspaper journalist. She wants to do an article on the clothing drive. I told her we would love to have an article done to spread the word, but that we didn't want our names on it. She said she would leave our names off of it, and I'm sure she will, but—"

"Knowing Genavieve, the news about the drive, and who started it, will be all over the school," Miranda finished.

As if to prove her point, Toby walked up. "Heard you girls were working on some type of thing for the homeless people," he said, looking at Autumn.

Smiling ruefully, Autumn said, "Yes, we are. Though nobody was supposed to know who was starting it."

Toby cocked his eyebrows. "Why not? I think it's a great thing that you're doing. Why don't you want the credit for it?"

"Well," Autumn fumbled for an answer. She was pretty sure Toby was not a Christian and she wasn't sure how to answer his question. She looked to the other girls for help.

Miranda stepped in. "Because we're Christians, we want the glory to go to God instead of ourselves. The only reason we're doing this is because we love God, not because we are so good, so we can't really take credit for it."

Toby shrugged. "Whatever." Then turning back to Autumn, he said, "Hey, if you need any help on the day of the drive, I could volunteer. Unless it's just a Christian thing."

"Oh, we can use all the help we can get. We're not sure about the time yet, but we'll know that by tomorrow."

"Great. Just let me know and I'll be at your service." Then, with a grin, Toby was gone.

As soon as he was out of hearing range, the three girls turned toward Autumn with big smiles on their faces.

"I think he likes you, Autumn," Savannah said.

"That's nonsense," Autumn retorted. "All he wanted to do was volunteer to help."

"Toby Fraser, volunteering to help at a clothing drive for the homeless?" Kaylee said. "I don't think so. You'll remember that he was one of the ones who complained most about having to go to the homeless shelter."

"And he's the kind who doesn't like to associate with 'God people,'" Miranda added. "Normally, he wouldn't give a hoot to what we were doing."

Autumn rolled her eyes. "You're reading way too much into this. He just asked if he could help at the clothing drive and you're already assuming he likes me. Next thing you know, he'll talk to me at the clothing drive, and you'll be asking me if he's proposed yet."

They all laughed at that.

"So if we're finished discussing my romantic life," Autumn said, "we can get back to discussing the important details about the clothing drive." She took out her notebook. "I talked to Miss Marlin at the homeless shelter. She said she would help us out. Savannah talked to Principal Sterling and that's also a go." She turned to Kaylee. "Are we going to be able to make the posters at your house tonight?"

Kaylee nodded. "All the supplies are bought, and my mom is working on the cookie batter."

"Good. On the posters, we'll need to include that it's on Tuesday, December 20, and the list of things that they could bring. And that they can start bringing donations at . . . What time should we say?"

"How 'bout nine?" Miranda asked.

"Nine o'clock sounds like a good time to me, and then we could end at three," Autumn looked at everyone else. "Is that good?"

Everyone nodded.

"Okay, nine o'clock it is," Autumn said, jotting it down in her notepad. "Then any volunteers can come at eight thirty, so we can get organized and know who's doing what."

"Depending on how many volunteers we get, we can switch people out so there's not some people who sit around all the time, and others who work the whole time," Kaylee said.

"That's a good idea," Savannah said. "We should probably have one person just supervising, making sure everything runs smoothly."

"I vote Autumn for that job," Miranda threw in. "All in favor say 'Aye.'"

"Aye," Kaylee and Savannah said.

"It's unanimous," Miranda said with a grin.

"Hey!" Autumn said. "I don't think that was a fair vote."

"It was your idea," Kaylee said. "I think it's only fair that you're the one in charge."

"I guess I could," Autumn said, "but I still don't think that was a fair vote."

*****

Later, as Autumn and Savannah stood outside by themselves, Savannah turned to Autumn. "Tell me honestly," she said. "If Toby was interested in you, would you be interested back?"

"Well . . ."

"C'mon, Autumn," Savannah coaxed. "I'm your best friend. You can tell me anything."

Autumn sighed. "Okay. First things first, I'm not allowed to date yet nor am I interested in it. And if I was, Toby would not be my choice of guy."

"He's so handsome, though."

"Yes," Autumn assented, "he is handsome and a hotshot, he's a bully who thinks he's so much better than everyone else, he thinks he can have every girl he wants, and he's just an overall jerk."

"Ouch." The voice came from behind where the girls were standing.

Autumn turned quickly and turned a very bright shade of red. "Toby! I'm . . . I didn't . . ."

Toby cocked his head. "Don't worry about it, Autumn. Everything you just said is true. I've just never heard it put quite that way." He shifted his backpack on his shoulder. "Anyway, I just saw you two over here and thought I would let you know that I was serious about helping out at the clothing drive, so you just let me know when I need to be there. I guess I'll catch you later." Then he turned to leave.

"Toby," Autumn called after him. She almost turned to follow him, but just then Kaylee's mom's vehicle pulled up to pick up the four girls.

As the girls walked up to the vehicle, Autumn muttered to Savannah, "Well, if you wanted me to get together with him, you might as well give it up now."

Chapter 11

Kyle looked at where Riana lay sleeping on a blanket on the floor. It was far from the most comfortable place, but it beat staying on the streets.

It had taken a while, but Kyle had finally saved up enough money to rent a run-down apartment room. He hadn't been sure if he would be able to get a room because he was underage, but when he had come into the office to rent it, the slovenly dressed lady behind the counter had barely given him a second glance. She had just accepted his money and told him his room number.

As he had turned to go, she stopped him with the words, "Don't be late or Rudy will kick you out." She motioned to a buff man sitting in the corner of the room. Though he was half asleep, one could tell that he wasn't someone you would want to mess with.

Kyle made sure the rent was paid. There was no way he was letting Riana back onto the streets. She didn't deserve that.

Before he had come up with enough money to rent this room, Derek had made the offer of him and Riana staying in one of the gangs houses. There were several that had extra rooms where they could stay. If Kyle hadn't had to think of Riana, he would have jumped at the offer. But he did have to think of his sister, and he didn't want her to be hanging around those kinds of people. There was a nagging thought at the back of his mind that told him that he was becoming just like the kinds of people he didn't want her to be around, but he quickly shoved that thought away. He was only doing what needed to be done to take care of Riana.

Glancing at the time, he realized that it was time to meet Derek and the gang. He had no time for trivial thoughts like that.

*****

"What do you mean, you lost him?" Daniel Quinn glared at the officer standing in front of him.

They had searched the alley and at first, they had thought it was clean, but just to be on the safe side, they had brought in the drug dogs, who went crazy. Only through that they had been able to find the well-concealed drugs behind the brick in the wall.

They had finally found Kyle again, and Daniel Quinn put one of his officers on the job of following him to see if they could bust this drug outfit.

"I followed him for a couple of blocks, but then he disappeared," the nervous-looking officer explained. "I waited there for quite a while, thinking he would come out of a hiding place and I could keep following him, but he never did. I looked all over the place, but I couldn't find him."

Daniel sighed and ran his hand through his hair. After his run in with the kid on the street, he had thought that he was a rookie, which would make this job easy. Just follow him and you can get the whole gang.

Annoyed, Daniel turned to the officer. "Well, Stanley, get back to work."

Stanley turned to go, but then hesitated. "I did find out something, sir."

"This had better be good," Daniel muttered.

"I think I found where the kid lives. Before he realized I was following him, he went to some apartment on the south side of town. He spent some time in there, then came out, and shortly after, I lost him."

Daniel instantly was on edge. "Maybe that's where the drug dealers are staying."

Stanley shook his head. "I don't think so, sir. When the kid was leaving, I seen a face looking out of the window. It looked like a young girl." He shrugged. "It was kinda hard to tell because the window was dirty, but she didn't look much older than my daughter who's ten."

"Good work, Stanley," Daniel said. "Now, all we need to do is watch the apartment and we can nab them."

*****

Kyle was getting nervous. He had seen the police officer following him once, and it seemed that there was always someone outside the apartment. Maybe he was just getting fidgety, but he was almost sure that they were plain clothes policemen. The closer it got to the big deal, the more nervous he got. He wanted in this thing, wanted the money it would give him and Riana, but . . .

He glanced out the window. Sure enough, there was a man seated on a bench on the other side of the street.

Overhead, dark clouds filled the sky, threatening to give them a blizzard.

Chapter 12

Plans for the clothing drive were coming together nicely. Kaylee's dad had put an announcement on the radio two times. Posters were hung all over town. Many people had volunteered to help out.

School finished in a blur. Several times, Autumn had tried to talk to Toby, but the time never seemed right.

The day of the clothing drive was cold and blustery, snow blowing with each gust of wind. All the volunteers arrived bundled up.

Autumn scanned the crowd of volunteers, mostly students and a few adults like Principal Sterling and a few teachers. Toby was not among them. Her heart sank. She had hoped that today she might be able to apologize. She sighed. Her words must have kept him from coming. Oh well. There was work to be done.

"Okay, everyone," Autumn said. "First things first, we'll need to get some tables set up. I would like to have two tables over there for clothes, two over there for the blankets and pillows, two over there for shoes and socks, and two over there for toys or any other items people may have brought. We'll need to have someone at the door greeting people. And we'll need to have one person stationed at every table to make sure that only the designated items are put there. There will need to be other people ready to bring items to the back once the tables get too full. We will keep items separate back there too. And we will need a couple of people back there going through everything, making sure that there is nothing that needs to be washed and checking for any junk that needs to be trashed." Autumn stopped to take a deep breathe. "There aren't enough jobs for everyone, so we'll take one-hour shifts. Let me know once your hour is up, and then I will get you a replacement."

Principal Sterling cleared his throat. "In the office, there is coffee, hot chocolate, and donuts for those of you who are waiting."

This announcement was greeted with a round of applause.

Volunteers were quickly put to work, while the others with no jobs sat down to wait until their shifts.

Autumn surveyed everyone working. Things seemed to be rolling smoothly.

"Hey, Autumn."

"Toby," Autumn said, turning to face him.

Toby grinned. "Sorry I'm late. Our car got stuck on our way out of the driveway. Dad came home with his Duramax to pull us out."

Autumn joined him in laughter.

"Anyway, I'm here to work," Toby said. "What do you need done?"

"Well, right now, we have all the jobs covered. I'll let you know when we need someone to switch out."

"Great," Toby said, turning to go.

"Wait, Toby," Autumn said.

He turned back.

Autumn shifted uncomfortably. "I-I'm sorry about what I said the other day. It was unkind and I shouldn't have said it."

Toby shrugged. "Everything you said is true."

"True or not, I shouldn't have said it. Some things are better left unsaid."

"It's not a big deal, Autumn," Toby said, his grin returning. "I've heard a lot worse." He sobered again. "Anyway, it's given me a lot to think about."

This time when he turned to walk away, Autumn didn't try to stop him. Silently, she said a prayer. "God, please continue to work in Toby's life. Help him to find that You can help him improve."

*****

The day flew by. Many people came and went, bringing tons of donations. Autumn was busy a lot of the time, making sure people only had to work their one-hour shift, keeping everything organized, and making sure everything was running smoothly.

At one point, Savannah caught up with Autumn. "It's your break time, girl."

"There's still some stuff to do—"

Savannah held up her hand to interrupt. "Stop! Just because you were nominated as the person in charge, doesn't mean that you are the only one who can handle it. I can take over with this for a little while, and you can go get some coffee and donuts and sit down for a little while."

Autumn had to admit that sitting did sound really good right now. "Okay, I'll take a little break. But I'll be back soon."

As soon as Autumn walked into the office where the coffee and donuts were, Kaylee came up to her. "Savannah hired me to keep you in here for at least an hour, so sit down." She pointed to a seat. "Do you want coffee or hot chocolate?"

"Hot chocolate."

"How about a donut?"

"That sounds good." From her seat, Autumn looked at Kaylee. "You know, I could get that myself."

"Sure, you could," Kaylee said, as she brought over the hot chocolate and donut. "You could also run this whole clothing drive on your own if you wanted to, but we all agreed to go in this together, so it's only fair that we all help each other out instead of letting one person run themselves ragged."

"I'm not running myself ragged," Autumn protested.

"Just rest for a while, okay?"

*****

Three o' clock rolled around and volunteers slowly started going home. Autumn, Kaylee, Miranda, and Savannah were stuck in the back, organizing things.

Looking at the stacks and stacks of things, Miranda moaned. "This is going to take ages to get boxed and handed out."

"Well, once we finish up with this, we can go home," Autumn said. "Miss Marlin will be coming here to help us sort everything out, and box it all up. She'll know better what to include in each box. Hopefully, we can get it all done in one day. Then, we'll help with distributing later."

Miranda sagged in her chair. "I am pooped."

"Me too," the other three chimed in.

"You know, that means our day was a success," Kaylee pointed out. "If there wasn't enough work to keep us busy, we'd be very discouraged instead of tired."

Miranda groaned. "Only you, Kaylee, only you, could see something on the bright side of being exhausted."

Savannah started to giggle. Soon, all the girls were laughing so hard that tears were streaming down their faces.

"My, you look like you're having fun," came a voice from the doorway. "What's so funny?"

Autumn looked up from where she was sprawled on the floor. "Oh, hi, Mom," she glanced at the other girls who were now trying to hold in their giggles. "It's nothing really."

Mom cocked an eyebrow. "Really?"

"I think we're all just a little overtired," Miranda said.

"Well, then it's time to get you girls home."

As they were walking to the car, Mom asked, "So how was the clothing drive?"

"Oh, it was great," Autumn said. And once again, they launched into the story of their day.

Chapter 13

Riana didn't stir when she heard Kyle get up. The alarm clock that Kyle had recently brought home proclaimed that it was ten o' clock at night.

Kyle quickly put on his jacket and shoes and crept to the door. He slipped out of the door, closing it quietly behind him.

As soon as the door closed, Riana stood up and went to the window. She watched until Kyle disappeared around a corner, then she, too, hurried out the door. She got to the corner just in time to see Kyle round another corner.

Kyle's brisk pace soon left Riana breathless, and she had to be very careful, because every now and then, Kyle would stop abruptly and look around. A few times, Riana was almost sure he had spotted her, but he kept going.

Slowly, they were getting into a worse part of town, and Riana was starting to feel very nervous. Where was Kyle going? What had he gotten himself into?

Suddenly, Kyle turned into an alleyway. He ducked behind a dumpster, squatted behind it, and glanced around.

Riana quickly hid behind a bush, where she waited to see what Kyle would do next.

After waiting a couple of minutes, Kyle got up, looked around once more, and trotted to the door. He knocked twice, paused, then knocked three more times. The door opened a crack and then closed behind him.

Riana wasn't quite sure what to do. She desperately wanted to believe Kyle wasn't doing anything wrong. Her mind turned, trying to come up with a plausible reason for his secrecy. Maybe he just had friends he didn't want her to know about. But even as she thought it, she realized that that couldn't be it. From somewhere, Kyle was getting money, and lots of it. There was some other reason for that, and there was only one way to find out what it was. Taking a deep breathe, she peaked around the bush. All the windows were closed with no way to look in. But if she got closer, she could find a way to peak in. And if not, she would just knock on the door.

Suddenly, hands grabbed her from behind. One hand clamped firmly over her mouth, while the other held her tightly around the waist.

Riana struggled and kicked, panic taking over.

"It's a girl, sir," a low voice said.

"Ten-four," crackled a voice over a walkie-talkie. "Keep her secure."

"Affirmative."

Riana continued to struggle, trying to get free.

The voice whispered in her ear. "Don't worry. I'm not going to hurt you. Just stay calm. I'll let you go as soon as this is over."

Though Riana wasn't sure if the voice was telling her the truth, she realized that there was no use in struggling. He was too strong. She stopped squirming and instead started looking around. From her spot behind the bush, she could see other dark forms, getting in position around the house.

Suddenly, the stillness of the night was broken by a bullhorn. "This is the police. We have the house surrounded. Come out slowly, hands in the air."

Chaos erupted inside the house. Banging around, yelling, and cursing could be heard. The door flew open and silhouetted against the light from inside, Riana saw a big black man, waving a gun in one hand, and holding Kyle as a shield with the other.

"Touch me, and this boy gets killed," the man yelled.

Even from where Riana was, she could see the terror in Kyle's eyes.

What happened next was all a blur. From out of nowhere an officer appeared tackling the man holding Kyle. As he fell to the ground a gun went off, and Kyle fell with him. People were streaming out of the house, more gunshots were fired, police officers appeared from every direction.

A silent scream formed in Riana's throat. 'Get up, Kyle, get up,' she ordered silently, but he didn't listen. With a sudden burst of energy, Riana broke free from the arms that held her and ran to her brother's still form. Tears streaming down her face, she grabbed Kyle's hand and shook it gently, willing him to open his eyes. Kyle's face was a deathly white, and a red stain was forming on his shirt.

Riana was vaguely aware that someone was screaming, a long anguish-filled scream. Only when hands gently pried her away from Kyle did she realized that she was the one who was screaming.

Chapter 14

Autumn leaned her head against the seat of Miss Marlin's car. The girls had spent the whole day handing out boxes from the clothing drive to homeless people, and she was exhausted.

"Have you regretted starting the clothing drive, yet?"

Autumn opened her eyes and looked at Miss Marlin. As usual, the stern woman was completely serious. But having spent a lot of time with her lately, Autumn knew that behind her composure, Miss Marlin was a very caring woman.

She grinned. "Not at all. I am very tired, but just thinking about those people's faces when we handed them their boxes," she shook her head, "it was worth every bit of work we put into it."

"And do you think the other girls agreed?" Miss Marlin asked.

"Yes," Autumn said without hesitating.

"Then, perhaps, we can work together on some other projects in the future."

"That would be great," Autumn said. "You have my number, so anytime you need help . . ."

Miss Marlin smiled one of her rare smiles. "Thank you, Autumn. Not many young girls would be willing to do what you four have done. It has done my heart good to see it."

Just then they pulled up to the hospital.

"Are you sure it's okay for you to be dropped off here?" Miss Marin asked. Kaylee, Miranda, and Savannah had all been dropped off at their homes, since they lived in town, but Autumn's house was out of town, so she had suggested being dropped off at the hospital.

"Yup," Autumn said. "Mom's shift ends at 10:30, so I'll only have to wait fifteen minutes. We've done this before. The hospital management doesn't mind since I'm older and not going to get in the way."

"Okay," Miss Marlin said. "Thank you again."

"Thank you, Miss Marlin, for helping us out," Autumn said, as she grabbed her backpack and headed to the door.

As she entered the hospital, Autumn waved at Mary, the secretary.

"Hello, Autumn," Mary said. "Waiting here 'til your mom's shift ends?"

"Yup," Autumn said.

Just then, Mom came from the back. "Autumn, I'm glad I caught you. We just had a couple of ambulances called out. It sounds like we're going to need all the doctors that we have on this one. Call your dad and see if he can come pick you up." With that, she rushed back behind the swinging doors leading to the emergency room.

Autumn watched Mom hurry off. Already in the distance, she could hear the sirens of an approaching ambulance. Turning to Mary, she asked, "Can I use your phone? My cell phone died."

Mary clucked her tongue. "Youngsters these days and their gadgets."

Autumn couldn't help but laugh. "The way you talk makes you sound ancient."

"I am ancient. Don't you know that fifties are ancient?"

Again, Autumn laughed. "I guess I was left out of that news flash. Anyway, my cell phone is only for emergencies." She grinned sheepishly. "Of course, Dad likes to remind me that it helps nothing if it's dead."

The two laughed, but then Mary sobered. "You're going to need to wait a bit to use the phone. The ambulance is here. Make sure you stay out of the way."

Autumn quickly moved to the side of the room.

The door burst open and paramedics rushed in, a stretcher between them. Autumn didn't get a good look at the patient but could see a big splotch of blood. The stretcher was quickly wheeled to emergency room door and disappeared behind it, leaving a calm behind.

Then the door again flew open, but this time instead of paramedics, a young girl and a police officer came in. The girl ran to the door of the operating room, but before she could go in, the officer stopped her. The girl kicked and struggled, a high-pitched scream coming from her tightly closed mouth.

Both Autumn and Mary hurried over to see if they could help. The officer seemed relieved, when Mary lifted the girl from his grasp and wrapped her in a tight hug.

"What happened, officer?" Mary asked.

The officer scratched his head. "As far as I can tell, the boy that was shot must be her brother or something. She was there when it happened. She must be in shock because she hasn't spoken a word since it happened. She wouldn't answer any of my questions. Just shook or nodded her head."

"Well, we'll watch out for her now," Mary assured him.

"Much obliged." With that the officer turned and walked away, happy to be getting back to his normal duties.

"Well," Mary said, still holding the struggling child. "Let's get this youngster calmed down."

It took a few minutes to get the girl to stop squirming. Her eyes had a wild look in them, like a trapped animal. She didn't once open her mouth.

Autumn stared at the girl. She looked so familiar. Where had she seen her before? Suddenly it hit her. "Mary, I know her!" she said.

Mary frowned. "How do you know her?"

"Well, not really know her," Autumn corrected. "I've seen her once. When our class went to the homeless shelter to serve Thanksgiving dinner, she was there with her brother. He must be the one who . . ."

The girl looked up at Autumn and tugged at her sleeve. Her eyes silently pleaded Autumn for an answer to her many questions.

"What do you need?" Autumn asked.

The girl shook her head and pointed at her mouth.

Suddenly it dawned on her. "I don't think she can talk," Autumn said, turning to Mary.

"It's possible that the trauma caused her muteness," Mary suggested. "It often happens when someone goes through something very traumatic. They call it voluntary muteness or something like that."

"Maybe," Autumn said, "but she never said anything at the homeless shelter either."

Turning back to the girl, Autumn asked, "Can you talk?"

The girl shook her head.

"Do you know how to write?" This question came from Mary. A nod.

Mary scurried over to her desk to get a piece of paper and pencil.

Then came the list of questions. "What's your name?"

"How old are you?"

"Where do you live?"

"Where are your parents?"

They found out that her name was Riana, she was twelve years old, she lived on the south side of town with her brother; her parents were gone. She didn't specify where they were gone, if they were dead, or if they were just gone.

At the end of her answering questions, Riana wrote one questions down. "Is my brother going to be okay?"

Mary's eyes became misty. "The doctors are doing their best to help him."

Here Riana only nodded.

After a while, Mary went back to her desk to work on stuff there. Autumn sat with Riana, both absorbed in their own thoughts.

Chapter 15

"Autumn!" The voice jerked Autumn awake. "Autumn, what are you still doing here? You were supposed to call Dad and see if he could pick you up."

Trying to remember where she was, and why she was here, Autumn stared through bleary eyes at Mom. "What—" Then she remembered. She was at the hospital. She glanced at Riana who was sleeping beside her. "I'm sorry, Mom," she said, "but before I had a chance to call, the paramedics came in with a stretcher, and then a police officer came in with Riana," she motioned to the girl sleeping beside her, "and she was scared so I was going to sit with her for a while, until she calmed down, and then I must have dozed off . . ." Autumn's voice trailed off when she noticed Mom was smiling instead of looking mad.

"I'm proud of you, Autumn, for helping out in a situation like this."

By now, Riana had woken up and was looking at Autumn inquisitively.

"Riana, this is my mom," Autumn said. "She's a doctor here. Mom, this is Riana. It was her brother who was shot."

Mom squatted beside Riana. "Well, Riana, it looks like your brother is going to be okay. He's asleep right now, but you'll be able to see him in the morning."

A look of relief crossed Riana's face.

Mom stood up and continue. "But for tonight, you're going to need a place to stay. Officer Quinn," Mom motioned to the doorway, where the same officer that had brought Riana in was standing, "will

52

bring you to a foster home where you can stay the night, and then you can come see your brother in the morning."

Riana shrank back against Autumn, a look of terror filling her eyes. Frantically, she shook her head.

"Couldn't she come home with us?" Autumn asked. She was filled with sympathy for the young girl. "At least she knows me a little, instead of having to go to complete strangers."

Mom looked at Officer Quinn.

"I think I can arrange that," he said. "Let me see what I can do."

Riana seemed to hold her breathe until Officer Quinn returned. With a smile, he said, "It's settled. She will be going to stay with you for tonight."

*****

It was past midnight when they got home and got Riana bathed and into bed. After they were sure she was asleep, the Shays sat down in the living room to discuss the day.

"What exactly happened to her brother?" Autumn asked.

"It was a drug bust," Mom said. "Along with Riana's brother, there were two others who had been shot and are in the hospital." Pain filled Mom's eyes. "He's so young. He couldn't be much older than you, Autumn, and already he's involved in drug dealing." She shook her head. "It makes you wonder, if maybe somebody could have done something to prevent him getting involved in it."

"I saw him," Autumn interjected quietly.

Mom's head jerked up. "What?"

"He's the one I told you about that had the cut on his face at the homeless shelter. I wouldn't have known except that I remember seeing Riana."

Dad looked at Autumn. "Well, now, we know the reason you needed to pray for them."

"But what if I was supposed to do something more?" Autumn looked at her parents with tortured eyes. "Like you said, maybe I should have done something to prevent this."

Mom moved close and put her arms around Autumn. "Honey, you prayed. That is the most important thing you could have done. Perhaps your prayers are what stopped the bullet from hitting his heart." She looked at Dad and explained, "Had it been any closer to his heart, he would have died, but instead he lives. We never know what our prayers prevent or help along with."

Autumn lifted her tear-filled eyes. "What's going to happen to them?"

Dad sighed. "Riana's brother—"

"Kyle," Autumn interjected. "Riana told me his name is Kyle."

"Kyle will be tried and most likely sent to juvenile detention." Dad shook his head. "Riana will be put into a foster home. Maybe she'll have a chance at adoption, but being as old as she is, likely she won't be."

"Couldn't we adopt her?"

There was silence, as Autumn's question hung in the air.

"Autumn," Mom said, "it takes a lot of paperwork and time to even get into the system and be able to foster children, much less be able to adopt."

"Yes," Dad agreed, "and with your mom and me both having busy jobs, we just don't have time for that. It takes a lot to get into that, and I don't know that it would be good for Riana to be in a family like ours. With Mom working irregular shifts at the hospital . . ." He let his sentence hang in the air.

"I grew up like that and I turned out just fine," Autumn said quietly.

"But we have no idea what type of past Riana has had. She may not be able to handle it like you could."

Tears again filled Autumn's eyes. She blinked them back fiercely, frustrated at herself for being so childish.

"You're exhausted, Autumn," Mom said. "I think you need to go to bed and get a good night's rest."

Autumn nodded, bid her parents good night, and went up to bed.

As soon as Autumn had gone up, Andrew turned to his wife. "What do you think?"

"It's against my better judgment to even think about it. It wouldn't work. We're far too busy to consider taking someone in." Maureen shook her head. "But honestly, when I saw Autumn and Riana asleep in the emergency room, my first thought was that Autumn missed out on a lot by not having a little sister. Finding out that she had been living on the streets. Well, let's just say that I was thinking about it even before Autumn mentioned it."

"Then it sounds like we need to be praying about this," Andrew said. Without further hesitation, the two knelt, echoing the prayer that was being prayed in Autumn's bedroom.

Chapter 16

Riana woke with a start. Where was she? Where was Kyle? Panicked, she sat up quickly and looked around. A strange bedroom met her gaze. She was in a pretty room, painted green with pale pink accents. The bed on which she was laying had a pink bedspread with green swirls on it. On the floor, on a pullout bed with matching blanket, was Autumn. Suddenly it all came back to her. Following Kyle, seeing him shot, being brought to the hospital, then going home with Autumn.

Riana closed her eyes. Memories of last night seemed like a bad dream. Slipping quietly out of bed, she walked out of the room. Unfamiliar sights met her in the hallway. She had been so exhausted last night that she hadn't paid any attention to her surroundings. She walked down the hallway. In the doorway to a cheerful yellow kitchen, she saw a lady working. She started to slip out quietly, but it was too late. She had been spotted.

"Good morning, Riana," the lady said cheerfully.

Riana wracked her brain. Who was this lady? She must've met her last night because she obviously knew who Riana was, but Riana couldn't remember who she was.

"Are you hungry?"

Riana shook her head.

"Well, sit down anyway."

Riana obeyed.

The woman wiped her hands on a towel and sat down across from Riana. "I just called the hospital to check up on your brother. They say he's doing fine. He lost a lot of blood, so he'll need to stay in the hospital for a while, so he can rebuild his strength. But he's going to be okay."

Just then, Autumn walked into the room. "Good morning, Mom, Riana," she said sleepily.

"Good morning, honey," Mom said. "I was just telling Riana that her brother is going to be okay. He'll need to stay in the hospital a while to regain strength, though."

A look passed between Autumn and her mom. There was something more they weren't telling her, Riana was sure of that. If only she had a piece of paper so she could ask. She grabbed Autumn's hand and looked up at her, letting her eyes ask the question.

Autumn sighed and turned to her mom, who nodded.

Autumn knelt beside Riana. "Riana, do you know what your brother was doing at that house?"

Riana shrugged. It was something illegal, she had figured out that much, but there was no way to tell them that without something to write on.

Again, Autumn sighed. "It looks like he was helping to distribute drugs."

Drug dealing? Riana shrank back in horror. She should have known, should've realized, but she had always reasoned that he would never fall into something that bad. Yes, something illegal, but not something where he was putting other's lives in danger. Kyle had always told her that drugs where awful for you. He had warned her that she was never to even think about trying them. Even cigarettes, which were a lot more common had been forbidden to her. And here he was distributing drugs? It didn't make sense.

Tears filled Autumn's eyes. "Riana, I'm sorry. But if Kyle was helping distribute drugs, he will go to jail."

Riana nodded. If they expected her to cry, they were wrong. She wouldn't cry. Not now, not here. Deep down she had known this was going to happen.

Again, Autumn and her mom exchanged a look.

"Well, let's eat breakfast," Mom said. "The social worker will be here in half an hour to pick you up, Riana, so we need to eat, so you're ready for when she comes."

For a moment, horror filled Riana. Social workers, the ones that separated you from the people you love. Then a dry thought filled her head. She was going to be separated from Kyle anyway. He would be going to jail. She still felt numb, but she made sure she didn't let Autumn and her mom realize that.

Later, after she went to wash up, she heard them talking.

"I'm surprised that she didn't really react to her brother being put in jail," Autumn said. "She was more surprised at the fact that he was dealing drugs than that he was going to jail."

"I noticed that, too," Autumn's mom said. "She also didn't react much to the fact that the social worker was coming. Yesterday, she seemed terrified at the thought of going to a foster home, yet today, it didn't seem to faze her."

Riana laughed wryly. If only they knew. Yesterday, she had shown her feelings to them only because she was exhausted. When you lived on the streets, you learned to hide them. The only person who could tell what Riana was thinking was Kyle.

Well, thought Riana, it was time to learn to live a whole different life. Kyle was no longer there to protect her. She would have to fend for herself. If only she could see Kyle before she struck out on her own.

Chapter 17

Beep, beep, beep.

The sound woke Kyle up. He looked around. The sights and smells brought back unpleasant memories. Memories of when he was a little boy and had found out that his baby sister would never talk like normal children would. And the time, when later, he had learned that his mother had lung cancer. But, Kyle shuddered, the last visit . . . the last visit was the worst. He had never told Riana about it. She didn't need to know. It would only hurt her, and she didn't need to be hurt again. Because that last visit had been to see Daddy. It had been several years back. He had heard about a bar fight that had taken place not far from where he and Riana often took refuge from the weather. According to the rumors he heard, a man named Richard Bennet had been severely wounded. He had gone to the hospital just to be sure. The man on the hospital bed had barely resembled the man he had once called Daddy, but it was him. If he had been conscious, Kyle would have had a lot of things to ask him. *Why did you leave us? Why didn't you let us know where you were? How could you leave with Mama dying?* It was probably a good thing he hadn't been able to talk to him.

Kyle had left full of angry feeling for the man who had deserted them. A few days later, he heard that Richard Bennet had passed away.

And now Kyle was the one in the hospital.

*****

Autumn and Mom waved goodbye as the car pulled out of the driveway, taking Riana to a foster home. Autumn couldn't keep tears out of her eyes, as she turned to Mom. "She's going to be so alone."

"Autumn, we did what we could."

Anger flared up in Autumn. "No, we didn't! We could've let her stay here! I've always wanted a little sister."

"Autumn." The stern tone of Mom's voice told her she had gone a step too far.

Taking Autumn by the shoulders, Mom said, "Look at me, Autumn."

Autumn reluctantly looked up at Mom.

"Talking to your father or to me in that tone of voice is unacceptable. No matter how you feel about something, you should never use that tone of voice with me."

"I'm sorry, Mom." Autumn hung her head. "It just slipped out."

"It's okay," Mom said. "But you need to learn to guard you tongue. And your attitude," she added meaningfully. Glancing at her watch, she said, "I need to get to the hospital. I called them to let them know I would be late today, so I may be home a little later than usual."

That ended the conversation, but it kept going on in Autumn's mind. Surely, there was something more they could do! The day dragged by so slowly. Autumn paced the floor, then stared out the window alternately. What was Riana doing now? Was she feeling lost and alone? How was Kyle? How would he react to going to jail?

The phone rang, breaking into Autumn's thoughts. "Hello," she said, trying to pull her thoughts together.

"Hi, Autumn," Savannah's cheerful voice greeted her. "I called earlier this morning, but your mom said you were still sleeping. I guess that's what Christmas break is for, right?" She laughed.

Autumn tried to join in, but it sounded fake even to her own ears. "Yeah, I was really tired."

"No kidding. You do sound tired. Did I wake you up?"

"No," Autumn assured her quickly. "Yesterday was just a long day."

"Well, you need to wake up before this evening," Savannah said. "Miranda is throwing a Christmas party this evening. She asked me to let you know because she's super busy getting things ready."

Savannah chattered on about the party, but Autumn stopped listening. When she could, she broke in. "Actually, I don't think I can make it."

"What?"

"I'm really beat, Savannah. Tell Miranda I'm sorry."

"Now, don't you go slipping back into that 'I feel so sorry for the homeless that I can't have any fun' mood," Savannah said. "We just got over that."

Unable to hold them back, Autumn burst into tears.

A shocked silence came from the other end of the line. Then, cautiously, Savannah said, "Autumn. Are you okay?"

Once Autumn's tears subsided to sniffling, the whole story of last evening spilled out.

"Oh, Autumn," Savannah said. "That's awful. Don't worry about not coming to the party. I'll let the girls know you can't make it. And I'll be praying."

Those simple words spoke encouragement to Autumn. "Thanks, Savannah."

As she hung up, Autumn felt a twinge of guilt. Savannah's last words were a wake-up call. "I'll be praying."

Even feeling as she had today, Autumn, instead of turning to her heavenly Father, had only wallowed in self-pity and sorrow.

Dropping to her knees right then and there, Autumn poured out her heart to God. "Father, I'm sorry I forgot to pray. Please forgive me for leaving off the most important thing. Please help Kyle and Riana . . ."

Chapter 18

S upper found all three Shays unusually quiet, each one absorbed in their own thoughts.

Suddenly, the ringing of the phone broke the silence.

"I'll get it," Dad said, shoving his chair back.

Dad's voice traveled back to Mom and Autumn.

"Hello."

"This is the Shay residence."

"Yes, sir."

"I see."

"I will call you back. Thank you for letting us know. Goodbye."

Mom and Autumn looked at Dad expectantly.

"Well," Dad said. "That was the social worker, calling about Riana." He took a big bite of mashed potatoes.

"Andrew!" Mom scolded when he picked up another forkful. "We want to know what they said."

"You do?" Dad asked innocently, then laughingly put his fork down. But then he sobered. "Riana tried to run away from her foster home today. She was climbing out the window when the foster mother walked in. They had been planning to take her to the hospital to see Kyle, but instead they took her to the social services building. They decided they didn't want to take her in if she was going to continue to try to run away."

Mom shook her head. "She hasn't even been there a whole day and already she tried to run away?" She clucked her tongue.

"Wait a minute," Autumn said. "If the family that took her in doesn't want her, what's going to happen to her?"

"Well," Dad said, "that's the reason the foster home contacted us. The police officer told them that she seemed to trust you, Autumn, so social services decided to ask if we would take her in. If not," Dad shrugged. "They'll most likely send her to an orphanage."

Orphanage. Pictures of a cold stone building with ragged, under-fed children being forced to work hard all day long ran through Autumn's mind.

Dad, seeing the horrified look on his daughter's face, said, "Orphanages these days are really well-cared for. The only thing is that these children don't get the love of a father and mother."

Autumn grinned ruefully. Of course, she knew Dad was right. Orphanages weren't really like that, but that's what came to mind when someone mentioned them.

"What do you think?" Dad asked Mom.

Autumn jerked her head up. Where they really considering it? This afternoon, after a long talk with God, she had resigned herself to the fact that they weren't going to take Riana in. She had figured it wasn't God's will. And now, there was the possibility that it would happen after all?

"Well, it would be a lot of work," Mom said. "Getting approved for foster care takes a lot of paperwork and time. And it's been a long time since we've had someone as young as Riana living here. But I believe this is God's answer to our prayer last night."

"I agree," Dad said. "As soon as we finish supper, I'll call them back and let them know we are willing to take her in."

"Wait a minute," Autumn interjected. "What prayer?"

"The prayer that was asking if God would want us to take Riana in."

Autumn shook her head in disbelief. "I thought you didn't want to take her in." Turning to Mom, she asked, "Why didn't you tell me this earlier?"

"I didn't want you to get your hopes up," Mom replied. "We wanted to make sure it was God's will before we let you know. And even if it wasn't God's will, that wouldn't mean we didn't care about her." She added, "And that definitely does not excuse your attitude earlier."

"I know. I really am sorry about that."

Supper was finished in record time, and Dad went to the phone to call social services back. A few minutes later, he was back in the kitchen where Mom and Autumn were doing dishes. "It's all settled. There's some paperwork that needs to be done before she can settle here permanently, but since tomorrow is Christmas Eve, they've decided to let us pick her up tomorrow and do the paperwork after Christmas."

"Great!" Autumn said. She grinned. She was going to have a little sister! Silently, she offered up a prayer of thanksgiving to God.

Chapter 19

Autumn woke up early the next morning. Christmas Eve had always been an exciting day for her. That was the day that her family opened gifts and spent time together. When she was younger, she always woke up early because of anticipation of gifts, but today was different. It seemed God had given them all a Christmas gift today.

Looking at the time, Autumn saw it was only seven o' clock. Dad said they could go pick Riana up at nine. Two whole hours to wait!

To make the time go faster, Autumn went to the kitchen and began rummaging through the cupboards. Maybe she could make waffles for breakfast. She needed to do something.

Gathering all the ingredients quickly, Autumn started mixing it up.

Before long, Mom joined her in the kitchen. "What are you making?"

"Waffles."

"That sound good," Mom said. "I'll make pudding to go with it."

Autumn grinned. Mom's home-made pudding was the best.

After she had put the first waffle into the waffle-maker, Autumn began making coffee. The tantalizing aroma of waffles and coffee brought Dad out of his room.

"Smells great in here," Dad said.

As they sat down, Autumn said, "You know, I was thinking—"

"Oh dear," Dad teased. "That's always a bad thing."

Autumn laughed, then continued, "We don't have any gift for Riana. It would be awkward if we exchanged gifts in front of her, so either we have to do it before we go get her or we need to get her a gift."

"We're a step ahead of you," Mom said with a smug smile. "We have a gift for her."

"You do?"

"As long as you don't mind that we give her one of your gifts," Dad said. "If you don't want to give up one of your gifts, then I don't know what to do."

"Oh, that's perfectly fine," Autumn assured them. Just then a thought hit her. "Will she be coming with us to the gathering tomorrow?"

Every Christmas Day, the whole Shay family got together at Grandma and Grandpa's house for a family gathering.

"Of course," Mom said. "She's part of our family now."

*****

Autumn waited impatiently for Mom and Dad to get back with Riana. Why was it taking so long? Did something go wrong? Maybe it had been decided that she couldn't come after all, until all the paperwork was done Or maybe she had decided that she didn't want to live with them after all. Or maybe she had run away again. Or—Autumn stopped herself. She was being silly, and she knew it. If something had went wrong, Mom and Dad would have called her. Still, she couldn't help but pace the living room floor until she heard the garage door opening. They were home!

Riana looked a bit uncertain as she walked into the room. Mom and Dad followed close behind.

"Welcome home, Riana," Autumn said, resisting the urge to hug the young girl.

"Well," Mom said, "do we want to open the gifts now?"

Dad smiled. "Now is as good a time as ever."

Gifts were soon piled on the living room floor.

Riana sat stoically, watching the Shays without an expression on her face.

As they all sat down, Dad turned and addressed Riana. "Riana, like we told you before, we want you to become a part of our family. So, as the newest member of our family, you get to open your gift first." He handed the astonished girl a brightly wrapped present.

At first, she just stared, not knowing how to react. The only person who had ever cared enough to give her a gift had been Kyle. Why would these strangers be so nice to her? All she is is a homeless girl. It didn't make any sense. Suddenly, she realized that all their eyes were on her.

"Open it," Autumn urged. She was just as curious as Riana about what was in the package. What could Mom and Dad have decided to give her?

Slowly, Riana began pulling the wrapper off. It seemed almost a waste to tear it off. At the top of the package was a pretty notebook with a set of pens beside it.

"So you can talk to us," Mom clarified.

Underneath it was a fuzzy blanket, the softest Riana had ever seen. And underneath that was a beautiful necklace. Riana pulled it out and stared at it in awe.

*****

Autumn recognized the necklace as soon as Riana pulled it out of the box. It was the necklace Autumn had been wanting for a long time. It wasn't very expensive, but just more than she had been willing to pay for herself. But she felt no envy that her parents had given it to Riana instead. Looking at the look of joy in Riana's face, she knew she would rather go without any presents than miss this priceless moment.

*****

That evening, Riana approached Autumn, notebook in hand. It was time to get some answers.

"Why?"

Autumn looked at the notebook, then back to Riana. "Why, what?"

In answer, Riana picked up the necklace that hung around her neck and gestured to the room, then wrote on the paper. "Why would you do all this for me?" Looking at the younger girl, Autumn carefully weighing her answer. "We did it, because we love you, Riana."

Again, "Why? You don't even know me."

"Because," Autumn hesitated, "Well, do you remember the story that Dad read to us before we ate lunch?"

Riana nodded. The story had been about a baby born in a stable, because the city was so crowded none of the inns had room.

"Well, that baby that was born in the story," Autumn said, "was Jesus. He came to earth to be born for us. Then when He got older, He started preaching and helping people and making sick people well again. He loved everybody so much that He wanted to help them. He didn't care if they were rich or poor. The people that most people avoided He helped, because He loved them. But some people got mad at Him. He was preaching to them about God and they didn't like that, so one day they killed Him."

Riana shuddered. Death had been a big reality in her life. She had watched her mother fade away and die. And then from living on the streets, she had seen a lot more of it. Suddenly, she didn't want to hear the rest of the story. If this Man was so nice and if He helped people who nobody else liked, people like her and Kyle and all the homeless people, why would anybody kill him?

Seeing Riana's look, Autumn quickly went on. "But that's not the end of the story. You see, Jesus didn't stay dead. He was in the grave for three days, but then He rose from the dead. He came back alive because He is God. Death couldn't keep Him there."

That didn't make much sense, Riana thought. The whole story confused her, and it didn't really answer her question. "What does that have to do with you helping me?"

"Well, you see," Autumn went on. "Because Jesus helped people so much, He wants us to help others. We love others because He loved us so much. Because we follow Him, His love is in our hearts, and we want to share it with everybody just like He did. Does that make sense?"

Even as Riana nodded her head yes, she thought that it didn't make any sense at all. Because a Man Who was nice to people died but then wasn't dead after all, they were nice to her. But if they wanted to believe that, they could. Weird as the story was, Riana couldn't help but think about it as she lay in bed, waiting for sleep to come. When she drifted off to sleep, she dreamed of a Man walking around, talking to all the homeless people and healing the ones who were sick.

Chapter 20

Kyle woke up with a start. Riana was sitting by his bed with a big smile stretched across her face. He had tried asking the nurses about her, but they had never given him a straight answer about where she was. "She's being well taken care of," is all they would tell him. Now as he looked at her, he could tell it was true. Her neatly combed wet hair and her clean and radiant face told him that she had bathed before coming. She was wearing new clothes that fit perfectly and around her neck hung an elegant necklace. And she looked very happy.

"What are you doing here?" Kyle asked gruffly. Seeing her so well-taken care of reminded him of what a poor job he had done in taking care of his sister.

Holding up a notebook, she wrote, "Autumn and the doctor brought me."

"Who's Autumn? Why are you with a doctor? Are you sick?" Kyle waited as Riana bent over the notebook to write her reply.

"I live at Autumn's house. The doctor is her mom. They are both very nice. No, I am not sick."

"So you're staying with Autumn and a doctor?"

A nod.

"Where'd you get that necklace?"

"Autumn's dad gave it to me for Christmas."

Kyle lay there, silently taking all this information.

Riana started writing again. "Kyle, do you know who Jesus is?"

Kyle jerked. "Why do you ask?"

"Autumn told me a story about a Man named Jesus. It was very confusing." Riana waited for Kyle's answer. If ever she was confused or wondering about something, she always asked Kyle. He was very smart and had an answer for everything. She wasn't prepared for his outburst.

"Don't you ever listen to such nonsense. It's crazy! Just foolish superstition. You remember what I've taught you about superstition."

Riana nodded, startled. Somebody had once told her that she was going to have bad luck because a black cat crossed her path. She had been terrified until Kyle had set her straight. Bad luck was not something that came from black cats or breaking windows or anything stupid like that. But this didn't sound at all like the type of superstitions that Kyle had told her about. It was just a story. Why would Kyle react like he did?

"Now, I don't want to hear any more nonsense like that, okay? You just forget you ever even heard anything like that."

Riana nodded. But, though they could talk about something else, she wasn't going to forget the story so easily.

"What does your room look like?" Kyle said.

The rest of the conversation went on like that. Kyle asking questions, Riana writing the answers down.

*****

"It's time to leave, Riana," Autumn said, poking her head into the room a few minutes later. "We need to get to the social services office. We have an appointment there soon."

Riana rose to leave, but before Autumn could follow her, Kyle said, "Miss Autumn?"

Autumn turned back, startled that he even knew her name. "Yes?"

"I don't want you talkin' to my sister about Jesus."

"What?"

"I don't want you to talk to my sister about Jesus or God or any of your pathetic religion. It's all a waste of time, and my sister doesn't need to have anything to do with it. You're all a bunch of hypocrites, anyway."

"Are we?"

This time it was Kyle who was taken off guard. He was quiet for only a moment, then he sneered. "Yeah, you are. You all feel guilty for a moment and then you forget about us."

"Sure," Autumn said. "We're all hypocrites. That's why after our class went to the homeless shelter, I felt almost sick. After seeing you, with that big cut on your face, your poor sister, and all those other homeless people, I couldn't focus on anything else. My friends can verify that. It took me a while to get back to normal life. My friends and I then decided to do a clothing drive. The day you were shot, we had just finished handing out all the food and clothing that we had gotten during the drive. I was dropped off at the hospital because my mom works here. She was one of the doctors who operated on you. Riana was brought in, too, and I recognized her as the one I saw at the homeless shelter. She was nearly hysterical because she witnessed the whole thing. It took a while to calm her down, but she did eventually. We ended up taking her to our house for the night because she didn't like the thought of going with a social worker. Then, when she tried to run away from the foster family she was staying with, we offered to take her in. She came to our house on Christmas Eve, and I sacrificed some of my Christmas gifts because I wanted Riana to feel like part of our family. We took her shopping today to get some clothes that fit her well because mine were too big for her. We've only had her at our house for a few days and already she feels like family, and my heart aches for her because she's going to lose her brother or at least it will feel like it. But, yes, we're all hypocrites."

Autumn turned and walked away, leaving Kyle in stunned silence. So that's why she looked so familiar. She was the girl from the homeless shelter. He shook his head in amazement. It was a wonder she even recognized him.

Then another thought hit him. She said that Riana had witnessed the whole shooting. Why had he not been told that? Riana hadn't even told him. What was she doing there? Had she followed him? Perhaps. He had been a bit too preoccupied on the way there.

Derek had blamed the whole bust on him. Kyle's thought drifted back to that fateful night.

*****

Kyle had been late. It had taken Riana a long time to fall asleep. At least he thought she had been asleep. He was in a hurry because of that and had not been as careful as he should have been.

He had reached the house safely, gotten inside, and started working, loading bags into specific containers. If they could smuggle all these drugs to a different location where a big buyer awaited them, they would be rich. Kyle remembered thinking how lucky he was that Derek had included him in this. It showed he trusted Kyle. But his moment of joy disappeared as a bullhorn broke the silence.

"This is the police. We have the house surrounded. Come out slowly, hands in the air."

Derek's gaze jerked over all the people there and landed on Kyle. "You fool!" he hissed. "You led those police here."

"I didn't." Kyle protested, but Derek wasn't listening.

Without a word, Derek grabbed Kyle, holding him like a shield in front of him. "You messed this up for all of us and now you'll protect me." He jerked open the door, keeping Kyle in front of him, and made a run for it. The rest was a blur to Kyle. There were gunshots and complete chaos. Then there was stab of pain in his shoulder, and then everything went black.

And Riana had seen that all? He shuddered at the thought. He found himself glad that Autumn had been there for Riana. Well, he thought quickly to justify his thinking, he wouldn't want Riana to be alone. Even if it was a religious person.

Chapter 21

Autumn stared blankly out the window as they drove to the
social services office. She mentally shook her head. Why was
Kyle so adamant about people not caring? He had had that
attitude when she had seen him at the homeless shelter. Autumn
was now slightly embarrassed at her reaction to Kyle's accusation.
It sounded like she was bragging about how caring she was. The
shocked look on Kyle's face had made her feel satisfied at the time,
but she realized now that she hadn't reacted in the most Christian
way. And right when she was trying to prove that Christians weren't
hypocrites. *Way to go Autumn*, she thought wryly.

After she had rounded the corner, going out of Kyle's hospital
room, Autumn had almost run into a police officer. He had given
her a friendly grin, and she kept going, but it had hit her hard. That
police officer was there to guard Kyle so he didn't make contact with
any of the gang members or try to get away, she realized.

"Here we are," Autumn's mom said, to no one in particular.

Riana tensed up. What if something went wrong and she
couldn't go home with Autumn and her family? She quickly pushed
the thought out of her mind. Everything would go fine. She schooled
her features, careful not to show any of her feelings to the two sitting
in the front of the car.

"Well, hopefully this doesn't take too long," Mom commented.

The office building was old and looked in need of repairs. A
frazzled-looking secretary directed them to a door with a name tag
that said "Miss Fin." "She's taking care of the Bennet file."

The Bennet file. How impersonal that sounded. Couldn't they at least use first names? Autumn thought. *That would sound a bit more personal.*

They were met by a stern-looking lady with gray hair and glasses propped on the edge of her nose.

"I'm Miss Fin." The lady wasted no time. "You are the Shays?"

"Yes."

"Good. Let's get to business. I need the names of everyone in your family, age, and occupation of each. We will need to do a background check on each of you, so if you have any criminal records, now would be the time to say so. Here are the papers explaining the terms of agreement. Read them very thoroughly and sign at the bottom. Because of the circumstances of this case, we are going to expedite this, so it won't take long to process this information. Do you have any questions so far?"

"Yes, I do," Mom said, glancing toward Riana, who had asked permission to go sit in the waiting room. "What can you tell me about Riana's past? We've asked her some questions, but she answers them very briefly."

"Well," Miss Fin answered, opening the file on her lap, "Riana was born on May 12. She is twelve years old. Kyle is three years older. His birthday is," she scanned the pages quickly, "December 30. He'll be sixteen years old."

Mom shook her head in disbelief. "So young," she said quietly.

Miss Fin didn't respond to Mom's comment but went on. "I'm sure you've already figured out that Riana can't speak. They realized she had a damaged vocal cord when she was three years old. From the looks of it, she didn't have any formal education because of that."

"No formal education?" Mom asked. "She knows how to read and write."

Miss Fin shrugged. "I don't know how she learned because we have no record of her ever being in school."

"Kyle probably taught her," Autumn interjected.

Again, Miss Fin shrugged and went on with her dialogue. "Their parents divorced when Riana was, let's see, four. Melanie Bennet, their mother, developed lung cancer because of excessive smoking and passed away when Riana was seven years old. Because we couldn't contact Richard Bennet, social services arranged to have the children put into a foster home, but before we could bring them there, the two ran away."

"Did you not look for them?" Autumn asked incredulously. "You just let them live on the streets?"

Miss Fin shrugged emotionlessly. "We did search for them but finding run-away children is nearly impossible. We never had much hope of finding them. Until recently, we had not heard of them." Looking straight at Autumn, she added, "There are so many children needing help, we may as well only help those who want it."

Autumn pressed her lips tightly together. If she had thought that things had felt impersonal before, that had been only a glimpse of what she saw now. Turning to Mom, she said quietly, "I think I'm going to go sit with Riana."

Mom nodded, and her eyes told Autumn that she understood.

As Autumn sat beside Riana, she was fuming. The way Miss Fin talked she may have been talking about stray dogs.

"Hi."

Autumn looked up into a pair of smiling eyes. The bright white teeth forming a smile were framed by one of the blackest faces that Autumn had ever seen.

"My name is Abby Stetor. Do you mind if I sit here?"

Autumn shook her head.

Still smiling, Abby sat down. "What's your name?"

"I'm Autumn, and this is Riana," She said, motioning to the girl sitting beside her.

"Oh, so this is Riana," Abby said cheerfully. "I've heard a lot about you Riana," she said turning to Riana. "Most of it good," she added quickly. "Are you from the family who's wanting to adopt Riana?"

Autumn nodded.

"So that means Miss Fin is taking care of your case."

"Yup." The disgusted look on Autumn's face was not lost on Abby, who laughed.

"Don't let Miss Fin's hard exterior fool you," Abby said. "She's not really as unsympathetic as you think."

"She doesn't even seem to care about the children she deals with!"

"That may be what it looks like," Abby said, "but I've seen a different side of her."

"Do you work here?" Autumn asked.

Abby nodded. "But that's not the only time I've seen a different side of her. You see, she was my social worker when I was a foster child."

Autumn's eyebrows shot up. "Really?"

"Yup. And, believe it or not, I loved her. She may seem dry and crusty and emotionless to you, but at that time in my life, she was the only person to show me any love, and I ate it up. And she was able to get me adopted into a wonderful family. I am treated exactly like one of the other family members." Abby laughed. "Most little girls want to be teachers or ballerinas when they grow up. But not me. I wanted to be just like my hero—a social worker. As soon as I was old enough, I started to work here with Miss Fin. And then I got to see yet another side of her. She can be, well, dry and crusty for lack of a better way to put it, but when she's dealing with children, she's the same person I remember from when she picked me up from my abusive home."

"But why would she need to change colors like that?"

"It's not exactly changing colors," Abby said. "It's hiding emotion. We come across so much stuff that brings us to tears. When I first started working here, I cried myself to sleep almost every night. But when we're working, we can't allow ourselves to bawl every time we feel like. We need to be calm and composed. Miss Fin's way of doing that is acting completely emotionless." Abby shrugged. "I try to be cheerful, but I'm afraid I sometimes get overly cheerful in trying to cover up my feelings."

"I guess I never thought of it that way," Autumn admitted.

"Most people don't. Well, I need to get back to work," Abby said, standing up. "It was nice meeting both of you. I hope your paperwork goes quickly." Then, with a smile, she was gone.

Riana held up her notebook. "She was nice."

"Yes, she was," Autumn agreed.

*****

Half an hour later, they were on their way back home. Mom explained what was going on with the adoption process, but a lot of it went over Autumn's head. But one thing she understood was that the 'quick' process of adopting Riana could take up to a year.

"What do they call slow, if a year is quick?" she asked.

Mom laughed. "Adoption takes a long time, Autumn, even when they hurry it as much as they can. They need to make sure that the child will get proper care, and everything has to go through the proper legal standards."

Autumn shook her head. "I couldn't stand it if it took longer than that."

In the back seat, Riana was sitting quietly, but her thoughts were anything but silent. *They are really going to adopt me,* she thought. It was all so confusing. Why? Why would they take in someone from the streets, when they could have easily chosen someone with a better background. Autumn had tried to explain it to her, but her answer had only confused her even more. And Kyle told her that it was all rubbish and not to listen to a word of it. But there was something different about this family. They had accepted her without question. The day they had taken her home, she was already an unspoken member of the family. They didn't treat her differently because of her handicap. Never before had anyone treated her this way, not counting Kyle. Was their religion junk like Kyle said? Or was there something to it? Riana closed her eyes. Never before had she had she had reason to question Kyle. He was the one who had taught her from when she was a little girl. And he was a good teacher. Always before, she had thought that Kyle must know everything, but was this something that Kyle didn't know? Were the Shays right?

Chapter 22

Kyle quickly got bored of the monotony of hospital life, but the boredom was nothing compared to the dread of what would come when he was released. He was no longer confined to the hospital bed, and he knew it wouldn't be long before they released him. The guard at the door was a constant reminder that as soon as he was out, he would be on his way to jail. Glancing toward the doorway, Kyle looked to see if the guard was there. If he was, he wasn't in plain sight. Not that it mattered much. Even if he tried to make a break for it, he wouldn't get far. He was sure the whole hospital staff had been alerted that he was a criminal.

A noise at the door caused Kyle to look up. In the doorway stood a tall, skinny young man. His sharp blue eyes seemed to see straight through Kyle.

"Who are you?" Kyle asked.

Moving closer, the man said, "Never mind who I am. I have a message from Derek."

Kyle cocked his eyebrows. "Aren't you worried about getting caught? You know I'm being watched, right?"

"The guard is taking his normal coffee break. He won't be back for about ten minutes."

Kyle didn't respond to that. "What does Derek have to say?"

"You need to listen and listen good." The young man leaned forward, and Kyle could smell beer on his breathe. "You rat on us, you tell them anything about any of the places you've seen, any of the people you worked with, and we will make your life miserable."

Kyle shrugged. With all his time to think, he had decided that the best thing to do would be to tell all. Derek had nearly gotten him killed and then left him to take the rap, and now he expected him to keep quiet about all that he knew. "How would he make my life miserable?" Kyle said. "I'll be going to prison after all. Unless he wants to come with me to prison."

"You think you're so smart, don't you?" the man sneered. "I don't know why Derek even trusted you. You're just a little twerp." He laughed a hard, bitter laugh. "Oh, we'll make you miserable, all right. Your sister Riana. The one that can't talk. Yeah, Derek's been watching her. Looks like she's enjoying living with the doctor, eh?"

Kyle's face went pale as he realized the implications of that statement.

The man laughed one more time. "When trial comes, you don't know anything. You hear?"

Kyle nodded. He glared at the retreating back, his blood boiling. Derek had claimed he would be part of a family. Some family this had turned out to be. "Family helps each other out." That's what Derek had said. But instead of helping Kyle out, Derek got him shot and left him to the police. Instead of helping him break out, he threatened his sister, the only person in the world who really cared about him. Yes, he would say what they wanted him to say. For Riana. But as soon as he got out of prison, he would find his revenge. One way or another.

Chapter 23

Autumn hummed cheerfully as she and Riana worked side by side, hanging up clothes. School started up in a couple of days, and Autumn was excited to see her friends again. She had told them about Riana over the phone but hadn't seen any of them in person since the clothing drive.

Riana, on the other hand, worked without a smile. She, too, would be going to school in a couple of days. The Shays had found a school where, besides the normal subjects, she would be taught sign language. Riana was less than thrilled. Things worked just they were now. Why did she need to learn sign language? But Mrs. Shay insisted that she needed it. Riana sighed inaudibly. How was she even to concentrate on school with Kyle in the hospital? He was getting better, but that was only a little comfort, for as soon as he was well enough to leave the hospital, he would be taken to the jail. Riana and Kyle didn't talk about it much during their daily visits, as though avoiding the subject would prevent it from coming. But they both knew it wouldn't be long. Soon, they would be separated by more than just a few miles. They would be separated by prison bars.

Riana blinked quickly to hold back her tears.

Autumn glanced at her, worry in her eyes. "Riana, are you okay?"

There was no use lying. Autumn had already seen her tears. Riana just shook her head. Inside, she was screaming, *Would you be okay?*

"Do you want to talk about it?"

Again, Riana shook her head. What good would it do to talk about it? It was only painful and didn't keep the day from coming.

Autumn reached over and gave Riana a hug. She then resumed hanging up laundry. But Riana saw that she too had tears in her eyes.

Chapter 24

Kyle hung his head as he was led to the front of the court room. He knew Riana was here somewhere, but he didn't lift his head to look. The past few days before the trial had been very hard, and he knew that if he saw Riana, he would start to cry again. And he wasn't going to cry.

The bailiff stepped in the door. "All rise. The honorable Judge Rawley presiding."

The judge walked in and seated everyone again.

The process dragged on. Kyle answered question after question. When asked how he pleaded, he readily answered, "Guilty." There was no way around that one. But that didn't satisfy the attorney. "How many people do you work with?" "What where the other people's names?" "Who is the leader?"

Kyle many times simply ignored the questions. There was no way he could answer them without putting Riana in danger.

After what seemed like forever, the judge banged his gavel down. "Kyle Bennet, you are found guilty, and sentenced to three years in juvenile detention."

Only three years, then, he could get his revenge on Derek and the rest of the gang. Only three years.

*****

Before Kyle was taken away, he was given one chance to talk to Riana. Her tear-streaked face broke his heart. Kneeling down and leaning close, so that his words were for her ears only, he whispered,

"You be a good girl, Riana. You'll probably be better off without me, anyway."

Riana shook her head frantically, a muffled sob breaking through her lips.

Kyle put his finger quickly on her lips. "Shh. It'll all be okay. You listen to what your new family tells you. You do good in school. You live a good life, you hear? Don't become like your no-account big brother."

Riana picked up her notebook and scribbled, "You're not no-account."

The police standing nearby cleared his throat. "It's about time to go."

Kyle nodded then looked at his sister one more time. "Remember, I love you Riana." Then he stood up. Without a word, he handed Autumn a folded piece of notebook paper. Then he looked at the officer. "I'm ready."

He was led away to the waiting squad car and helped in. As he turned one last time to look at Riana, she was crying on the ground without restraint. Autumn was holding her arms around her, also crying. Mrs. Shay knelt and placed her hand on Riana's arm. Kyle turned quickly away. Yes, Riana would be better off without him. She now had a family who would love for her and care for her in a way that he had never been able to. Even as he comforted himself with this, tears began rolling down his cheeks.

Chapter 25

Autumn was extremely curious about the paper Kyle had given her, but for the time being, she stuck it in her pocket. Right now, Riana needed her.

The ride home was very quiet. Riana's sniffling every now and then was the only sound. As soon as they got home, Riana raced up to her room.

Autumn started to follow her, but Mom held up her hand. "I think, she just needs some time on her own. You can go check on her later."

Autumn sighed, but she knew Mom was right. As she sat down on the couch, she heard a crinkling sound. Surprised, she reached into her pocket. Oh yes. The letter from Kyle. Opening it, she began to read.

> Miss Shay,
>
> I wanted you to know that I am grateful to your family for taking Riana in. She needs a good influence in her life, and, unlike me, I think you will be one. She's your family now. Somehow, I don't think you will have any trouble treating her like it.
>
> I have just one request. Don't bring Riana to visit me. She needs a clean break from our past. Bringing her to see me will only keep bringing the past into her life again. She doesn't need that.
>
> You can tell her about your God, you can make her a Christian, but please grant me this one thing.

You probably wondered why I got so riled up about you talking to Riana about God. Well, you might as well know. I've met quite a few hypocrites in my life. There were some ladies that came and visited us when my mom got sick. They preached at her, told her she needed to give up her "sinful life" and then she would be healed. They came three or four times, each time to get the poor sinners to repent, but never once did they try to help us out. We were obviously poor, and never once did they hold out a lending hand. So that's why I was skeptical when I heard you talked to Riana about God. But I can see that you're different. If Riana starts to follow your God in the same way you do, I will be happy.

Kyle

Feeling shocked, Autumn stared at the letter. "Mom," she said. "Look at this." Autumn handed the letter to her mom. "Kyle gave this to me before he was put into the car."

Autumn waited quietly while Mom read the letter. Her face mirrored how Autumn was feeling.

"Can you imagine how Riana would react if we told her Kyle didn't want to see her?" Autumn asked.

Mom shook her head. "She would probably try running away if we didn't take her to see him." Her eyes went back to the letter, and she shook her head again. "Those heartless ladies. Trying to 'convert' Riana's mom, yet never caring about them at all. No wonder Kyle reacted like he did when he heard we were telling Riana about Jesus." Her eyes shone with pride as she looked at Autumn. "He saw Jesus' true light in you, Autumn."

Autumn gave a half smile. Perhaps Kyle had seen Jesus in her, but what did other people see in her? Autumn's face colored a little as she remembered her hasty words that Toby had overheard. Did he see the light of Jesus in her?

Chapter 26

School. How Riana hated it. She couldn't understand why Mrs. Shay thought it was necessary for her to go. She had done just fine without it. She only went because they required it of her. She made no effort to talk to anyone, and if anyone talked to her, she pretended not to see them. If she could only get through the rest of the school year, she would be fine. And then maybe she could convince the Shays that she wasn't in need of special schooling.

The only thing that kept Riana from complaining, was the Shays enthusiasm. Every day after school, she was met at the door by Autumn and Mrs. Shay, if she was off duty, eager to see what she had learned that day. Then, later, at the supper table, she would have to repeat it for Mr. Shay. They tried to use the sign language they learned as much as possible. As much as Riana hated to admit it, the use of sign language really did make communicating easier.

There was only one other dim spot in her life. She had been with the Shays for a month and still no mentions had been made about visiting Kyle. She had asked one time when they would be going to see him, but Mr. and Mrs. Shay had exchanged a look, and only said, "I'm not sure." Autumn hadn't even looked at Riana, but only stared down at her hands. It made Riana feel uneasy. Was Kyle sick again and they didn't want her to know that? Was she not going to be allowed to see him? Were the guards beating him or something and they didn't want her to see him like that? Why were they acting so strange about it? It didn't take her long to figure it out though.

It was a cold, snowy afternoon, and Riana was sitting in the room she shared with Autumn. The Shays were fixing up a room for

Riana so they wouldn't need to share, though Riana honestly didn't mind sharing with Autumn. It was nice knowing she was not alone, and the room was bigger than the one she had shared with Kyle in their tiny apartment.

Riana was bored. Autumn wasn't home. She hadn't told Riana where she was going, just that she wouldn't be home until supper time. And now Riana had nothing to do. She had finished her homework, and the book she was reading didn't hold her interest for long. After a while of just staring at the ceiling, she decided to investigate and see what kinds of things Autumn kept in her desk. The top drawer held a bunch of odds and ends, some trinkets and souvenirs. It must be Autumn's junk drawer, Riana thought. The next drawer was a jackpot! It had chocolate and candy in it. Riana had seen Autumn eating chocolate before but had never asked where she got it from. This must be her secret stash. Riana lifted out a piece of chocolate. She knew Autumn wouldn't mind. But just before she took a bite, she noticed a piece of paper stuck underneath the chocolate. On the paper was writing that said, To Miss Shay. But it wasn't what it said that caught Riana's attention, but the handwriting. It was without a doubt, Kyle's handwriting.

Riana stared at it for a while. Why would Kyle have written a note for Autumn instead of to her? Well, there's only one way to find out, Riana thought. She picked up the paper and began reading. The words that rolled across the paper filled her with outrage. How could he! Kyle, her own brother, didn't want to see her! In fact, he had practically made Autumn promise she wouldn't bring Riana to see him! She threw down the paper. And he thought it would be good for her if Autumn taught her about God, the very thing that he had told her to forget about? Her first reaction was anger, but then hurt took over. She sank down onto her bed and cried. No wonder the Shays hadn't said anything about taking her to see Kyle. No wonder they avoided that subject at all cost. It was because Kyle had asked them not to take her to see them. She picked up the letter and reread it.

The story that Kyle told of the Christians coming to visit them was not something she remembered. The last words of the page jumped out at her. "I can see that you're different. If Riana starts to follow your God in the same way you do, I'll be happy."

Riana could see that the Shays were different. They were kind and had a joy that radiated from the inside. And unlike the Christians Kyle spoke about, they lived out what they taught. But did she really want to become like them? And did Kyle really not want to see her again, ever?

Again, Riana succumbed to her tears. In a rage, she threw the letter in the trash.

Chapter 27

The door clanked loudly, and Kyle heard heavy footsteps coming down the hallway. He didn't look up, expecting them to pass by. Instead, the jangling of keys stopped right at his cell. "Bennet, you have a visitor."

Kyle stood up reluctantly. Surely, the Shays would not have brought Riana. Not after he had specifically asked them not to. He followed the guard down the hallway to the visitor's room.

"Kyle." Autumn stood when she seen him approaching. "How are you?"

"You didn't bring Riana, did you?" Kyle demanded, ignoring her question.

"Actually, that's what I came to talk to you about." Autumn gave a half smile. "But I was going to be polite first."

"You didn't bring her?" Whether or not Autumn found it amusing, Kyle had to know.

"No."

"Then, I'm fine." Kyle sat down. "How is Riana doing?"

"Horribly." Autumn's answer was blunt. "She's having to adjust to a completely different way of life. She despises the classes she has to take for learning sign language. She tries to hide it, but I can tell. And on top of that, she misses her brother who doesn't want to see her."

"That's not true," Kyle protested. "I do want to see her. I'm just doing what's best for her."

Autumn shook her head. "You're not being fair, Kyle. You want Riana to become a part of our family, and even now, we are working

on adoption, but she will never accept us as her family if we're deny-
ing her the right to come see you."

"But—"

Autumn didn't let him finish. "You say you are doing what's
right for Riana, but you're wrong. With all the change going on in
her life, the last thing she needs is to be separated from the one person she trusts." Autumn stopped to take a deep breath. "Did anyone
tell you she tried to run away?"

Kyle shrugged. It sounded vaguely familiar, but he couldn't
remember what he had been told. "What about it?" he asked.

"I'm not sure where she was planning to go. She won't talk
about it, but I have a feeling she was planning to go back on the
streets again. You're trying to protect her from that life, yet back on
the streets is exactly where she might end up if you never let her visit
you."

"Time's up." A big guard stood beside them.

"We'll bring Riana by next Saturday."

It was a statement not a question.

Kyle nodded.

Autumn watched as he walked away, and the door clanked
behind him. Only when a hand was laid gently on her shoulder did
she look away.

"We should go home, Autumn," Miss Marlin said. Because Mrs.
Shay had been busy, she had offered to take Autumn to visit Kyle.

Autumn nodded wordlessly. She didn't trust herself to speak for
fear she would burst into tears. Suddenly, she was very tired.

*****

Back in the cell, Kyle sat down on his bed. He blocked out the
sound of the TV and the other boys staring and jeering. He knew
most of them didn't get visitors often, if ever, and he realized they
were probably jealous that he had gotten one.

Closing his eyes, Kyle leaned back against the wall. As much as
he hated to admit it, he knew Autumn was right. Riana was much
too stubborn for her own good. She would never understand the rea-

son for his not wanting to see her. And running away seemed to be just the kind of thing she would try. He shuddered at the thought of Riana trying to make it on the streets. It had been bad enough when he was there to protect her.

Kyle felt a small tinge of admiration for Autumn. She wasn't afraid to speak her mind. And already, in the short time that Riana had been living with them, she had gotten to know her pretty well. Riana was very good at hiding her feelings, so either she had gotten worse with that or Autumn cared enough to play close attention to her.

Kyle was feeling a mixture of emotions. Riana was coming next week. There was anticipation. He would see his little sister again! But then there was dread. How could he talk to his sister, the one he had betrayed? In trying to protect her, he had hurt her even more, and he could never forgive himself. Among these feelings was the deep anger he had hidden. Anger at Derek and the rest of the "family." Kyle slammed his fist onto his bed. A couple of the boys turned to stare at him, but he just turned his face. For Riana, for himself, he had to get revenge.

Chapter 28

"Thanks again for the ride, Miss Marlin," Autumn called as she stepped out of the truck. She jogged up the stairs and into the house. Tossing her purse on the living room couch, she headed into the kitchen. She plopped down at the supper table, where her family was already eating supper.

"Hi, honey," Mom said. "How was your day?"

"It was good." Autumn reached for the soup bowl. "I aced my history exam. Oh, and Toby stopped me at lunch today and asked me what our next project was going to be."

"Next project?"

"You know, for helping out the less fortunate." Autumn turned to Riana. "Maybe you have some ideas. You could probably help us out a lot, since you know what it is like."

Riana just shrugged and stared at her bowl.

Autumn raised her eyebrows and looked at her parents.

Mom shook her head and mouthed, "Later."

After Riana left the table, Autumn asked, "What's wrong with Riana?"

"I'm not sure," Mom said. "When she came down for supper, her eyes were red, but she wouldn't tell me what was wrong. She just ignored my question."

"How did your errand go?" Dad asked.

Autumn chuckled and shook her head. "I'm not quite sure. We didn't have much time to talk. He told me that what he was doing was best for Riana, but being me, I told him bluntly that he was wrong. I gave him a piece of my mind and didn't give him any time to protest when I told him that we were bringing Riana next Saturday." Autumn paused. "Are you going to tell Riana right away?"

"I think I will," Mom said.

*****

Riana stared at the wall when Mrs. Shay walked in. She knew it was coming. Mrs. Shay was going to try to get her to tell her what was wrong. Well, let her try. Riana didn't even turn when Mrs. Shay sat down on the bed.

"We're going to go see Kyle next Saturday."

Riana's head jerked up. She had been expecting an interrogation, not this.

"Visiting hours are between two to four, so I thought we'd plan to get there right at two, so you and Kyle can have as much visiting time as possible."

Riana just stared.

"Well," Mrs. Shay stood up to leave. "I just thought I'd let you know."

Riana grabbed her hand to stop her. Without letting go, she reached into the trash can to pull out the letter. She handed it to Mrs. Shay wordlessly.

Mrs. Shay's eyebrows rose. "Well, that explains some things. One of these days, we'll have to have a talk about not going through other people's things, but for now I'll just tell you that we've talked with Kyle, and it's been decided that you can go visit him."

Mrs. Shay left then, and for a long time, Riana sat staring at the ceiling.

Chapter 29

"Riana, it's time to go!" Mom called.

Autumn laughed. "Mom, she's already waiting for you in the car."

"Well, then, I guess we'd better get going. Did you grab the goodie basket?"

"Riana took it on her way out."

Mom grabbed her purse. "Okay, let's go."

The drive to the prison was too long for Riana. She drummed her fingers on the seat, bounced on her seat, and fidgeted the whole drive. More than once, Mom said, "Calm down, Riana." But that only lasted a little while, before she was back to fidgeting.

As soon as they were parked, she was out of the car and running to the building.

"Wait for us, Riana," Mom called after the disappearing figure.

"Don't worry, Mom," Autumn said. "They won't let her pass the front desk."

Sure enough, when they entered the building, Riana was pacing anxiously.

As they were led down a long corridor to the visiting room, Riana's pace slowed down. What would Kyle look like? Always before, he had been her anchor, but the day of the trial, he had seemed so lost. Would he still be lost? Or would anger have taken over? Riana repressed a shudder. Kyle didn't get angry very often, but when he did, it was not a pretty sight.

But the Kyle that met them that day was neither the forlorn Kyle of the trial or the angry Kyle. There was a look on his face that

Riana couldn't describe. It scared her a little. What had happened to the Kyle she knew?

Reading Riana's look of confusion, Kyle motioned to the seat next to him.

Autumn turned to leave, but Kyle stopped her. "I would like it if you would stay for a little bit. I have something to tell Riana and I would like you to hear it, too."

Riana fidgeted nervously.

Grinning, Kyle said, "Relax. I haven't been sentenced to the electric chair or anything like that. In fact, it's quite the opposite. I've been set free. Not literally, but spiritually." He paused as though not sure how to go on. "I've become a Christian, Riana."

A shocked look crossed Riana's face.

"I know. It seems I'm talking out of both sides of my mouth, right? I hated Christians because it seemed like they thought they were so much more righteous than we were. I used to hate Christians because of a few people who called themselves Christians but were only concerned about the outward appearance."

"After we met you, Autumn, I realized that maybe my idea of Christianity was not accurate. Maybe there are good Christians." He shook his head sadly. "But I was too stubborn to admit it."

Kyle paused for a minute before continuing. "After the drug bust, I became even more bitter than I was. I could think of nothing but revenge. In the hospital, every waking hour was spent planning how I could get back at the men who betrayed me. Instead of realizing that I was in the wrong and that I had brought it upon myself. I nursed a hatred for those who I thought had brought me into this and had left me to take my punishment on my own, and even threatened me to silence.

"But the things I've heard from you, Autumn, and from others, kept returning to me. Then, a couple of days ago, a family of singers came to the prison. The songs they sang were beautiful, and the words touched me as nothing else has. Afterward, I talked with one of the family. We talked for a long time and at the end, I accepted Christ." There was a glow in his eyes. Turning to Riana, he said, "I'm sorry for the mistakes I've made that have caused you suffering. I'm sorry for being such a bad example for you. I hope that you, too, will realized that you need Christ to save you."

Tears were glistening in his eyes, and he asked, "Will you forgive me?"

Tears in her own eyes, Riana nodded, and reached over to give her brother a hug.

Autumn stood once more and left the room silently. This time no one stopped her.

Chapter 30

"Hurry up, Riana," Autumn called from the bottom of the stairs.

Riana hummed as she leisurely pulled her jacket on. Slowly, she walked down the stairs where an impatient Autumn was waiting.

"Took you long enough."

Riana grinned unrepentantly and signed. "Are you in a hurry?"

Autumn gave a grudging smile.

The two girls were on their way to Toby's house, and Autumn was quite anxious to get on her way.

A lot had happened since last week's visit to the prison. Riana had talked a long time with Kyle and she, too, had given her life over to Christ. She had changed overnight, it seemed. Instead of dreading going to the special school, she was eager to learn. She read her Bible, a gift to her from the Shays. Her attitude at home had changed, too. Of course, there was still much that needed to be worked on, but she was well on her way.

As for Autumn, well, things had changed for her, too. Toby had stopped her on the way to her locker one day at school.

"Autumn, can I talk to you?"

Autumn was a little nervous. What could he want? She swallowed. "Sure."

"I was wondering," Toby paused as though unsure of how to proceed. "Ummm, what I mean is, I was serious about doing another project soon. I was wondering if we could meet with some people who were interested in helping out at my house this week."

Autumn let out the breath she hadn't even realized she was hold-ing. "That sounds good. Who were you thinking about inviting?"

"Well, of course, you and Savannah and Miranda and Kaylee. And you could invite whoever else you think would be helpful to the planning. And some of the guys from the youth group like Marcus and Stephen."

"Sure," Autumn said. "Just let me know when and I'll spread the word." She glanced at her watch as she pulled her books out of her locker.

"Ummm, Autumn."

She looked up to see Toby still standing there, his hands shoved awkwardly in his pockets. He cleared his throat. "I've been talking a lot with Marcus and Stephen. They've shown me a lot of stuff from the Bible that makes a lot of sense. It gives me a lot to think about. I'm still not quite sure about it all, but most of it makes a lot of sense." Another clearing of the throat. "One thing I've decided is that I need to focus on that for now instead of on things like, uhh, girlfriends and such. For now, anyway. You know . . ."

Autumn couldn't help the smile that spread across her face. "I'm glad, Toby! I've been praying for you, and I know that I'm not the only one."

A relieved look crossed over Toby's face.

The bell rang and as the two parted ways, the smile remained on Autumn's face. Not only was it great that Toby was seeking after the Lord, he also left the hope that one day . . .

Yes, Autumn mused as she pulled into Toby's driveway, a lot had changed. In some ways, things were still the same. Many of the chil-dren at school still had a bad attitude, there were still many homeless, and many who didn't know Christ. But God was working, touching one life at a time, using those who were willing to follow Him wher-ever He led.

About the Author

Lydia Wiebe lives in a small town in Texas with her mom and dad and four siblings: Lucas, Megan, Hannah, and Joshua. She is a teacher at a private school, a job that she loves. In her free time, she enjoys playing violin and piano, hanging out with friends and family, and playing with her two adorable nieces.

Lydia always has had a love for writing. She was always writing something whether it was a poem or a short story. She is thankful that her family is so supportive of all her writings.

CPSIA information can be obtained
at www.ICGtesting.com
Printed in the USA
FFHW021017250219
50648529-56060FF